Sandra's
survival of the baby...no help to
...a. He slammed his fist into the padded exam table. Why did she do it? Why did she panic like that?

He paused. In the deserted clinic, he heard a noise.

He followed it down the hall to the linen closet. From inside he heard the sound of frenzied weeping.

It could only be Julia. He'd thought she'd gone home after her mad dash from the surgery, but it seemed she'd gone into hiding instead.

He yanked open the door.

She sat in the dark closet on a laundry bag stuffed with soiled linens, crying into a towel. When the light hit her, she jerked her face up and hiccupped. She looked, he thought uncharitably, terrible. Her eyes were swollen, her nose was red, her cheeks mottled.

"Would you like to explain what the hell happened back there?" he barked.

She buried her face in the towel once more and sobbed. He recognized the signs of impending hysteria and knew that anger at this moment would only push her over the edge.

He reached down, gripped her by the arm, and pulled her upright. "My place," he ordered. "Get going. You have some explaining to do."

GW00690766

The Making of a Country Doctor

by

Patrice Moore

The Making of a Country Doctor

Cover Art by *Angela Anderson*

The Wild Rose Press
PO Box 708
Adams Basin, NY 14410-0706
Visit us at www.thewildrosepress.com

Publishing History
First Champagne Rose Edition, 2009

Published in the United States of America

Dedication

To Wendy and Patty, for all their staunch support—I love you ladies! And to Don, my hero for eighteen years and counting.

Chapter One

"Now Sara, we've gone over what you need to do to keep this baby as healthy as possible," said Ben. "But you're at risk for pre-eclampsia, so I can't emphasize enough how important it is to follow my directions."

"Does Sandra have the same condition?"

"It looks like she might. Honestly, Sara, did you and Sandra *plan* on getting pregnant at the same time?"

"No." Sara Johanson gave a shaky laugh. "But you know how twins are. We both wanted to start families. That's why it was so hard to lose the last baby."

Dr. Ben Taylor didn't have to be told. He'd known Sara and Gus since elementary school, had worked with them through their infertility problems. "Think positively, Sara. Every pregnancy is different."

"That may be so, Ben, but I'm counting on you. Please, just help me get this baby born. Losing the last one nearly killed Gus. He—he wants a child so bad, and so do I."

Ben patted her shoulder. He had to stretch to do this, as Sara was up on the exam table and he was sitting in his wheelchair. "Don't worry, Sara. We'll do our best to bring this baby safe into the world. But that's why I need you to follow my directions. No running a marathon, no weeding the garden, no splitting firewood, no digging ditches..." He smiled at her.

Sara smiled back. "Got it."

1

"You're twenty-four weeks along. When you hit thirty-seven weeks, I'm going to transfer you to the regional hospital. They're better equipped to handle high-risk cases, and as you can see..." He gestured downward. "...I'm not at my best at the moment."

Sara nodded. "I expected something like that." Her eyes were bright with unshed tears. "Thanks, Ben."

"You're welcome. Tell Sandra that I want to see her on Monday. Now go home before those hormones have you crying all over my shoulder and making Gus jealous."

After Sara left, Ben tried to wheel himself into the receptionist's area of his office by holding Sara's file in one hand and steering with the other. That didn't work, so he clamped the file between his teeth while using both hands to push the wheels of his chair. He ended up banging into the doorframe and dropping the file on the floor, where charts and papers fanned out. "Dammit," he muttered. "About the time I get the hang of this thing is about the time I'll no longer need it. Lisa...!" he called to his receptionist. "Would you mind picking up Sara's chart? I'll need to monitor her closely over the next few weeks. Schedule me to do a follow-up call next Friday..."

"I will. Ben, your Resident is here."

Ben straightened up. "Dr. Chambers? Good—someone to help us out. Please show her into my office."

He turned himself and wheeled down the hall to his private sanctuary. He had wanted to avoid the antiseptic environment often found in doctor's offices, so he hoped Dr. Chambers would be at ease here. Hardwood floors—he had removed the handsome Turkish carpet until he was out of the wheelchair—and walls lined with books, both medical and non-medical. Large rural prints on the walls. Behind his antique oak desk were large casement windows looking out on a stretch of green lawn that surrounded the medical facility in Jasper, Idaho, population 300.

Gypsy, his dog, thumped her tail in greeting. "Hiya, doll," he murmured, stroking her head. "Be nice to my new Resident, will you? I need her to stay. No no, put the paw down."

Ben rolled up to his desk, folded his hands on the surface, and waited.

Within a minute, Lisa's footsteps tapped down the old wooden hallway. "Right this way, Dr. Chambers," she said, and ushered the Resident into Ben's office.

Ben's eyes widened. While his office wasn't a typical doctor's office, Dr. Julia Chambers wasn't a typical senior resident doctor. Somehow the Portland City Hospital resident precept hadn't gotten around to mentioning that the resident they had sent to Idaho was beautiful.

"Ah, good afternoon, Dr. Chambers," he said, to cover his surprise. "Come on in. Forgive me for not rising."

"Pleased to meet you, Dr. Taylor—yikes!" She stared at Gypsy, who had risen politely to greet her. "Is—is that a wolf?"

"No, no!" Ben chuckled. He liked getting startled reactions to his enormous white dog. "She's a Great Pyrenees/Irish Wolfhound cross. Yes, she's big, but she wouldn't hurt a fly."

"Big! She's nearly up to my waist!"

"Just let her sniff your hand and she'll be your friend forever."

Julia ventured out a timid hand, and sure enough Gypsy nestled against her begging for pets. The woman still looked a bit alarmed, so Ben called the dog over to sit behind his desk.

"Sorry if she startled you," he explained. He held

out his hand. "I'm Ben Taylor."

"Julia Chambers." She placed her long, elegant hand in his.

If ever a woman looked out of place in a little place like Jasper, it was Dr. Julia Chambers. She had flawless rosy skin and her head seemed tilted back from the weight of a huge mass of luxuriant dark hair pinned up. Ben had a sudden, entirely unprofessional vision of releasing that hair and running his hands through it.

Good thing he was in a wheelchair.

Her eyes were a startling green—were they tinted contact lenses?—and looked guarded even though she was smiling. She had dark smudges under her eyes, as if she hadn't slept well for some time. Her slacks and thick wool sweater were tailored and urban.

"I'm pleased that you'll be joining us at the Jasper Medical Clinic, Dr. Chambers. Ah, may I call you Julia?"

"Of course." She pulled out the worn leather chair and seated herself. "If I may call you Ben, that is."

Ben smiled. "I don't think anyone here calls me Dr. Taylor. Even the little kids—children of my high school buddies—call me Dr. Ben. Of course, I grew up in this town, so that helps."

"You grew up here, and you're *still* here practicing medicine? How…cozy."

Ben frowned, not liking the slightly patronizing tone he heard in her voice. "I like to think of it as dedication. Loyalty, if you will. You see, the town banded together to put me through medical school. Naturally I'd never turn my back on them."

"Really. All the way through medical school?"

Ben nodded. "Todd Anderson, the older town doctor, was starting to think about retiring, but he knew there wasn't much of a chance of attracting a younger doctor to a small and isolated spot like this. I was in college and was interested in medicine. Dr. Todd talked me into going to med school with an idea toward taking over his practice when he retired. The town pitched in to cover the costs, and seven years later, here I am."

"Wow." Guarded respect crossed her face. "Quite an effort for a small town."

"Yes. But then last month I ran into a moose..."

"You ran into a *moose?*"

He grinned. "Yep. On my motorcycle. Took a nasty tumble and broke this leg so badly that I'm in the wheelchair for another month. So as you can see, we were in dire need of help. I appreciate your coming, Julia."

"A moose..." She shook her head with an amazed expression.

"There's a few around here. We're pretty rural."

"Yeah. I noticed."

That slightly condescending tone was back. "Do you have a problem working in a rural facility, Dr. Chambers?" he asked coolly.

"Uh, no. Of course not."

"Good. Because I think you'll find that the folks in Jasper are warm and friendly toward outsiders who are friendly back. Or, of course, you'll find they're stand-offish and cliquish to those who act the same. The choice is yours, Dr. Chambers."

He saw her eyes chill. "Thank you for the lecture on human behavior, Dr. Taylor."

He grinned. "Welcome to Jasper."

****

Julia exited the rinky-dink little hospital facility with clenched teeth. Of all the rustic backwater nightmares to which she could be assigned...well, Jasper, Idaho beat all.

The medical center could best be described as primitive. Oh sure, it was spotlessly clean, but it was located in an old converted building with worn floors and odd rooms. Nothing like the up-to-date facility in Portland, Oregon that she had just arrived from.

And the town...! No movie theater. No cafes. No boutiques. No mall. Hell, there wasn't even a Starbuck's in the two-block "business" district. She was surprised the place had a medical facility at all, except this Dr. Ben Taylor told her it was necessary in order to serve a large section of the extraordinarily rural county in north central Idaho. Julia was surprised to find a place so thinly populated in the continental United States.

She'd bet her medical training that all the people were nothing but...well, hicks. Backward, redneck, you-know-what-kicking hicks.

And she had to live here for three months.

But then she had wanted a place to hide her face and—hopefully—recover. That being the case, she supposed there were few better spots than Jasper.

She unlocked her car door and paused as she saw Dr. Taylor roll himself out of the facility in his wheelchair. That monster dog trotted next to him with her leash looped over the chair's handle. Dr. Taylor didn't see Julia because one wheel clipped a pole on his way out. The man had no experience with a chair, that was certain. She lingered a moment by her open car door, watching. She had to admit that he was rather good-looking—boyish face, curly brown hair, brown eyes, and an easy smile. Still, she hoped his bedside manner was better than his attitude toward "outsiders."

He didn't head toward a car in the parking lot. Instead, he simply rolled his wheelchair on the gravel sidewalk and headed out of town.

Since "town" was about four blocks long from start to finish, this didn't take long. He must live nearby. *Pretty handy if you can't drive your car*, she thought. She shook her head. Whatever.

Julia got in her car and drove three blocks to the little furnished rental house that was supplied to her as part of her residency arrangement. It was a single story, squat and old-fashioned, with nothing striking about it. She sighed as she got out and locked her car. The front porch actually had a rocking chair on it, like something out of Appalachia. Imagine.

God, her ex-fiancé wouldn't know whether to laugh or sneer if he saw her now. But fortunately— Julia firmed her lips—he *wouldn't* see her.

She unlocked the door, and the stray cat that seemed to come with the house instantly darted inside. "Oh, for cryin' out loud, you little beast, go back outside," she muttered. But the cat—an orange-and-white number—simply sat down in a corner with its tail curled around its feet and stared at her with large green eyes.

"Okay, fine. You can stay."

The cat blinked.

"I suppose you'll want me to get some cat food and feed you," she told him. She supposed he might be a useful diversion in this remote place. "Well, I'll add it to the grocery list." The list was getting longer as she thought of the staples she needed to purchase to stock the house.

The little house came equipped with everything she needed as far as furniture and appliances, but it was depressing and cheerless in the chilly April afternoon. Boxes of her possessions were scattered about. She hadn't yet figured out how to use the woodstove that seemed to be the only source of heat.

"A lot colder here than in Portland, isn't it, Cat?" she added, and leaned down to scratch the animal under the chin. An outsized rumble issued from the cat's throat. "And more primitive too. I hope I'm up to this."

She spent an hour unpacking boxes and putting clothes and books away. But her stomach was grumbling, and she knew that grocery shopping would have to be next on her list.

"Mmmmrrrr," said the cat. Surprised at his muffled tone, she looked down and saw a dead mouse hanging from the cat's jaws. Julia gave a small shriek. "Crap—get that thing out of here!" She opened the front door and shooed the cat into the night, wondering uneasily where in the house he'd caught it.

Okay, enough. She was getting out of the house, with its mice and cold air, at least long enough to buy some food.

She locked the door to her house and unlocked the door to her car. Though the town's modest-sized grocery store was mere blocks away, she figured she'd better drive because she anticipated a lot of purchases.

Parking in the store's gravel parking lot, Julia noticed a small diner across the street—Betty's Café. Impulsively she locked the car door and walked over. Might as well have a hot meal first.

Betty's was a no-nonsense place with Formica-topped tables and cracked-vinyl stools in front of the counter.

"Hi!" said a friendly gum-cracking waitress. "You here for dinner?"

"Please," said Julia. "Table for one."

"Why don't you join me instead?" said a voice.

Julia pivoted and saw Dr. Ben Taylor at a small table in the corner. He put down the newspaper he had been reading and smiled at her.

She nodded. "Thank you." She slid into the chair opposite him.

"I saw you park in the grocery store lot. Stocking up the house?"

"Yes. It's pretty bare."

"You locked your car door." He folded the paper and slipped it next to him in the wheelchair. "Don't

8

bother. You're not in Portland any more. If you're worried about car theft, put your mind at rest."

"Habit. Hard to break. It's going to take me awhile to get used to such a small place... thank you," she added, as the waitress handed her a menu.

"Ben, do you want me to hold your food back until hers arrives?" the waitress asked.

"Sure. Oh Sally, this is Dr. Julia Chambers. She's the new Resident at the medical clinic."

Sally cracked her gum and grinned. "Nice to meet'cha. Be back in a minute to take your order."

"So...how's the food here?"

"Surprisingly good. I eat here a fair bit. Cooking for one gets boring after awhile."

Julia glanced at his left hand and saw no ring. "I know the feeling. Can you cook in that wheelchair?"

"After a fashion. Since my accident, I depend a lot more on microwave meals. Yuck."

Julia nodded. "For my wheelchair-bound patients, I've found their entire houses are modified for their needs."

"I'd modify my house as well, but with luck it will be only another couple of weeks before I'm out of this thing. That's my hope."

"So what happened to the leg?"

"Snowy road. Big moose. Compound fracture of the femur and tibia. There was a lot of devitilised soft tissue and a lot of embedded road gravel because it was a high-velocity trauma."

Julia winced. "Ouch."

"Yes. The moose wasn't in such good shape either. Ralph Finnigan, the guy who found me, had to shoot the moose. I was knocked out, thankfully. He hauled me into the back of his truck and high-tailed me to Gritman Medical Center in Moscow."

"That's Moscow, Idaho?"

"Yes. It's a small university town with an excellent hospital, about fifty miles from here. Spent

9

a week dealing with the pain and learning how to use a chair." He grinned. "It certainly made me appreciate what some of my patients are going through!"

"Talk about a trial by fire."

"Yes. Anyway, the hospital in Moscow is where we send people whose health problems exceed our abilities. I'm a GP, so anyone requiring surgery or anything more complex than I can handle gets referred there."

"You do no surgery here?"

"As little as possible. Our operating room is small and we have no anesthesiologist. We recently purchase an anesthetic machine, so that's a help, but I prefer to send people to Moscow for anything complex."

"I see." *Backwater outpost*, she thought.

He must have read her mind, for his expression hardened. "I hope you're not having a hard time dealing with our limitations."

"Of course not." *Of course.* She had no desire to be here at all. "Rural people need healthcare as much as urban people."

"I'm glad you see it that way. You'll learn a lot here."

"I intend to."

"Good. I think you'll find, Julia, that our medical center has a different...well, I guess you could call it a different work ethic here than you might find elsewhere. The population is scattered, and I do a fair number of housecalls for elderly or handicapped patients. If you've spent most of your life in Portland or another big city, it's hard to comprehend just how spread out the population in this county is. Tamarack County has something like nine thousand people in an area nearly the size of Rhode Island."

Julia's eyes widened. "You're kidding!"

"I'm not. Now obviously I can't cover that entire

territory and still man the medical clinic—especially since my accident—but it gives you some idea of the scope we're working with. Fortunately we're not the only medical facility in the county, but we certainly cover quite a territory. It takes an extremely dedicated doctor to practice here. Doctors aren't attracted to such small places because of low pay." A quick smile came and went. "Except that my pay includes the prettiest scenery in the world, and some of the nicest people I've ever worked with."

Julia glanced out the window where the swollen clouds looked threatening. "I'll have to take your word on whether this place is as pretty as you say."

"Most of the snow just melted, so it will take awhile for the plants to poke out of the mud. Just wait a month or so. This is about the only place I've ever seen dandelions so big and beautiful that they're elevated to the status of landscape plant."

Julia shivered. "But it's so cold here still, and it's late April...!"

"Well, when it's cold, you just throw another log on the fire and cozy up to the woodstove..."

Julia chewed her lip and looked away. "Oh sure."

"What's the matter?"

"I, uh, haven't figured out the woodstove yet."

He stared at her. "So you've been without heat since you got here?"

"Yes."

"For heaven's sake, no wonder you don't like it here!" He slapped the table. "After dinner I'll go to your house and show you how to use it."

"You don't have to do that!" She gestured toward his wheelchair.

"Can't have my resident doctor freezing to death. After dinner, then." He gave a decisive nod.

The waitress arrived to take her order, and Julia realized she hadn't even glanced at the menu.

"Any recommendations?" she asked Ben.

"Try the soup. Betty makes all her soup fresh, so it's excellent."

Julia had her doubts that somewhere like Betty's Café could have *anything* excellent, but she ordered cream of broccoli soup and salad.

Once the waitress left, Ben leaned back in his wheelchair. "Are you unpacked yet?"

"Are you kidding? Not a chance." Julia folded her hands on the table and prepared for polite chitchat. "It's a nice little house," she lied. "I'm sure I'll be very comfortable there. So...what's Jasper like as a community?"

"Not bad. Of course, growing up here, I might be biased. Jasper is full of folks who can be gruff. They may take awhile to warm up to newcomers. But their hearts are big, and you couldn't ask for a better group in an emergency."

He embarked on a tale of a nasty winter storm where the power went out, and how the community banded together to help those who needed assistance. By the time he finished his story, the waitress had arrived with the food.

Julia picked up her spoon and took a tentative sip of the soup. She was starving by now, and would have eaten it even if it resembled paste. But the delectable taste spread through her and her eyes widened.

"My gosh, this is fabulous!" she exclaimed, and began to devour her food.

"You must have been hungry," commented Ben.

"Nothing since breakfast," she mumbled around a mouthful. She swallowed and said, "I'm surprised that somewhere like this would have anything good. I didn't expect much, but this soup is nothing short of gourmet."

Ben laid down his fork. "Look, Julia, I'll be blunt. You seem to have a problem being here in

Jasper. Why?"

Julia sighed and her delight in the soup fled. She looked out the window at the street running through the center of town. It was a bare, unattractive, no-frills type of town, with little or no effort to beautify it. In the darkening April evening, it looked bleak.

"Maybe I am," she admitted. She returned her eyes to Ben. "It's so different here. Much more than I expected. Even things like not having to lock my car doors or having you introduce me to the waitress. It's just...different."

"Maybe so, but it's not a *bad* difference. And as one professional to another, let me give you a bit of advice: don't let your attitude color your impressions of us. We're not Portland, or San Francisco, or Seattle, and a lot of people in Jasper are grateful for that. We don't have the amenities of the city, but we don't have a lot of the problems, either."

"Yeah, yeah." It was a phrase of frustration, and the moment it left her lips Julia wished she could undo it. Ben's expression cooled.

"Why on *earth* did you come here?" he asked.

There was no possible way she was going to tell him the truth. "I wanted a different atmosphere," she replied. She gave a self-deprecating laugh. "I certainly got my wish, didn't I?"

Ben gave her a long look, as if he didn't believe her. "Then what's your problem? Are you missing the amenities of the city?"

"Not yet."

"Do you think you'll be bored in your off-time?"

"I doubt it."

Are you worried that you'll be rubbing shoulders with a bunch of uneducated yokels?"

"No, of course not..." But her stained cheeks revealed that the last barb had struck home.

This Dr. Taylor was astute enough to realize the

truth, too. He lifted a glass of water to his lips. "I see. Tell me, Julia, how do you deliver a calf that's stuck?"

Startled at the odd question, she answered, "Well, I don't know…"

"How do you jump-start a tractor that's stalled?"

"I—"

"How do you take down a tree that's fallen in a dangerous position, without killing someone?"

"Well—"

"How do you make gourmet soup out in the middle of the howling wilderness?"

She glared at him. "Are you done yet?"

"Almost. My point, Julia, is that if you don't know the answers to these questions, I might just want to call *you* an uneducated yokel. These people know how to get by out here, and they know stuff you don't. Just because your degree came from fancy universities and their degrees came from the School of Hard Knocks doesn't mean you can look down at them."

She crossed her arms. "A little defensive, aren't we?"

"Only when the occasion calls for it." He took a bite of his dinner and chewed. "But we're going to have to work together for the next several months, and I won't have someone in my clinic with a snotty attitude."

"I don't have a snotty attitude!"

"Could'a fooled me. Okay, lecture's over. Finish your salad, and then we'll go figure out your woodstove."

Fuming, Julia attacked the salad, shoving it untasted into her mouth. "I need to go grocery shopping first."

"Fine. I can meet you at your house afterward."

The meal finished awkwardly. Julia paid and got out of there as soon as possible and walked across the street to the grocery store.

The grocery store may have been modest in size, but it was extremely well-stocked and rather cramped in an attempt to fit as many products as possible inside. Another surprise for Julia. She concluded that, since this store was apparently the only grocery store within fifty miles or more, it needed to be well-stocked in order to service the widely-scattered population. Even the prices were competitive, more or less.

Julia walked up and down the aisles with the cart, yanking items off the shelf in accordance to her list. Somewhere near the dairy section, with her hand on a carton of milk, she stopped and sighed.

Ben was right—she was taking out her feelings of shame and failure on this little town. Her trite statement in the restaurant—that rural people need healthcare too—came back to haunt her. That's why she's gone into medicine, wasn't it? To make sure that people who needed health care would *get* health care?

And there, in the dairy section, Julia had her epiphany and emerged from the grocery store with a better attitude.

She drove the short distance home. It was dark now, and she wished she'd left a house light on. Her rental was cold and dark and depressing. But she was here, and she might as well make the best of it. She began unloading the bags from the car. When she was done, she hesitated...and left the car unlocked.

While she started putting things away in the kitchen, she wondered what kind of doctor Ben was. A small smile cracked her face. After all, anyone who hung around Gypsy the Abominable Snowdog couldn't be all that bad. She hoped.

In ten minutes, she heard her doorbell ring.

"I'm afraid you'll have to push me up this step,"

he said, when she opened the door.

"No problem. Hang on."

Julia felt odd having her boss come into her home. The moment his chair was over the step, he wheeled himself inside and looked around.

"Brr. No wonder you're miserable. "You'll love this type of woodstove; it's as good as fireplace because you can see the flames." He grinned at her. "Very romantic, too."

She became guarded. "Let's keep this professional, shall we, doctor?"

"Sure. Whatever you say. Got some newspapers?"

Julia grabbed a stack from the pile inside the kitchen door that was left by the people who had moved out. Together they crumpled the papers and stuffed them into the stove. He showed her how to layer the fire with first small, thin sticks with larger sticks on top, the use of dampers and how to bank the fire for the night. Within ten minutes of his coming in the house, they sat back and watched the flames lick upward. Already she could feel the heat radiating from the cast iron.

"You've got at least a cord of wood outside," Ben told her. "More than enough to last you until the weather warms up."

"Seems like a pretty primitive way to get warm," commented Julia.

"I like to think of it as elemental. Properly used, a woodstove is very efficient. Plus the fuel is free if you cut it yourself."

"I can tell things will be more comfortable tonight," she commented.

"Spring takes longer to come here than it does on the coast," said Ben. "It can stay chilly into mid-June sometimes."

"In Portland, there are already blossoms on the trees."

"We have a more Rocky Mountain climate here."

Julia glanced out the window. "I'm trying not to think about this place as bleak and dreary."

"At the moment, maybe. The snow just melted, there's mud everywhere. Give it a month and you'll change your mind. The wildflowers around here peak in June, and they're spectacular. The lake is gorgeous, and it has some nice beaches for swimming. It's a good thing it's Friday. You'll have the weekend to look around Jasper and explore."

"I'll probably stay huddled inside, unpacking."

He glanced around the room. "Takes awhile to settle in, doesn't it? Hey, who's this guy?"

"A stray that seems to have adopted me." Julia nudged the cat with her toe. "I got some cat food at the store—let me get some for him." She opened the bag of cat food she had just purchased, and scooped some into a bowl.

An awkward silence fell as they watched the cat attacked the food with alacrity.

"What's his name?" asked Ben at last.

"I haven't given him one. I doubt I will, either."

"Why not?"

"Well, why should I? He'll stay here after I leave. No sense getting attached to him. Er, would you like some coffee?" she finally thought to ask.

"Do you have your coffee maker unpacked?"

"Are you kidding? What resident doctor doesn't live on caffeine?"

"Then sure."

He rolled himself into the kitchen as she set about making coffee. While the coffee machine wheezed and groaned as it started heating the water, Julia busied herself putting away the last of her groceries. But her conscience preyed on her. She poured the coffee and handed Ben his mug.

"Look, I owe you an apology for what we talked about over dinner," she said. "I *have* had a snippy

17

attitude since coming here, and it's not reasonable. I should be giving Jasper a chance." She managed a small smile. "I'm a city girl at heart, and can't help thinking that I'm in exile for the next three months. That I'm just marking time until I finish this rotation and can get back to Portland. But since I'm here, I've got to make the best of it. Having a working woodstove will help. Being cold all the time isn't the best way to keep a good outlook."

"I see." Ben looked thoughtful. He stayed quiet as he stirred sugar into the coffee. Then he nodded. "Well, it's big of you to acknowledge it. And that's all I ask—give Jasper a chance. I wouldn't stay here if I didn't feel an enormous affection to this area. The people make it all worthwhile."

"This place is pretty isolated. How do people make a living?"

"Some commute into Moscow or even Pullman, Washington. But not many. The roads get too treacherous in the winter. I've had to hammer a few people back together after their cars slid into ditches or trees after hitting black ice."

Julia sipped some coffee. "Does this area get plowed?"

"Sure. Jack Trelaine is our snow plow driver. Very dedicated. Most of the jobs in this town are related to logging, though. There's a sawmill on the north side of town. People either make their living in the woods or in the mill. Or in support services like restaurants or the grocery and hardware stores."

"What kind of hours do you keep? It doesn't look like my residency is going to be as intense as in Portland—no thirty-six hour stretches without sleep, that kind of thing."

"No. Not normally, at least. But like me, you'll be on call twenty-four/seven, because if something happens there's no other doctor to take over."

"Don't you ever get time off?"

"Yes. We have a circuit doctor who comes and stays on-call for four days every other weekend. His name is Dan Kendall, though we jokingly call him InstaDoc. Depending on our workload, you might get the same days off when Dan comes through. You'll find that Jasper is going to offer pretty intense GP training. Not intense in terms of hours, necessarily, but intense in terms of breadth of cases."

"Even though we're this far out?"

"*Because* we're this far out. I requested a Senior Resident to help me through until I'm back on my feet, but you can rest assured that by the time you go back to Portland you'll be as well trained a GP as anyone." He finished his coffee. "I should let you get back to unpacking. Thanks for the coffee."

"Thanks for the woodstove lesson."

"Remember, bright and early Monday morning."

"I'll be there."

She helped him down the step and watched as he rolled into the night.

Chapter Two

Bright and early Monday morning, Julia drove into the parking lot of the clinic. It would have been a matter of three minutes' exercise to walk, but she wasn't sure what to expect her first day on the job, and felt more prepared with her vehicle available.

The receptionist, Lisa, was filling in some forms when Julia walked in. "Good morning, Dr. Chambers," she said, smiling. "Have you met our nurse practitioner?"

"No, I haven't."

"I'll take you back and introduce you. She can show you around the clinic. Ben will be late, he's responding to a call."

The nurse, Adele, was short and middle-aged and comfortable. "Ah, there you are!" she exclaimed, holding out her hand. "I'm so glad to meet you. Ben is relieved that someone has come to help him, especially since he might be in that wheelchair for another few weeks."

"Nice to meet you," replied Julia. She liked the older woman immediately. "I hear you're the one who's going to show me around."

"Yes. We're small, so it won't take long. This will be your office, by the way."

It was small but functional. Julia dropped her purse on the desk and continued to follow Adele around the maze of rooms.

By the time Ben rolled in an hour later, Julia was familiar with the clinic and grudgingly impressed by the amenities. In addition to the three exam rooms, there were facilities for blood tests, microscopes for pathology studies, an X-ray machine, an ultrasound, an anesthetic machine, and a small operating room...not bad for a small town.

Ben came inside the door with Gypsy, the dog, leashed to his wheelchair.

"Does that dog go with you *everywhere?*" asked Julia, amazed anew at the dog's size.

"Sure. Another advantage of a small town clinic. Things are a little more relaxed. No, Gypsy, behave yourself," he added as the dog leaned into Julia's side as she scratched the dog's ears. "Just a warning, ears are her soft spot. She *loves* having her ears rubbed."

Julia laughed as the dog did, indeed, try to melt into her. "She's quite an animal," she admitted.

"Why Julia," said Ben softly. "That's the first time I've heard you laugh."

She sobered immediately and turned away, not wanting to acknowledge Ben's obvious interest in her. She hoped this wasn't going to be a problem.

She was here to learn. To train. To recover. That was all.

"Looks like you have your first patient in an hour," he commented. When she turned around, he was shuffling a chart, all professional. "Routine kid checkup and immunizations. There are some misconceptions and resistance to immunizations around here. I've been on a constant campaign to get people to vaccinate their children, so anytime I see kids for their shots I consider it a victory."

Julia suppressed a comment about any resemblance to third-world countries, and said instead, "How old are the children?"

"You'll just be seeing one, a boy who's six," replied Ben. "I'll sit in on the appointment because he knows me. Cute kid. I helped delivered him when I was an intern here."

He *was* cute. Avery Locke was a red-headed firecracker of a kid who faced his appointment with a gap-toothed bravery.

"Hello, Avery," said Julia. She sat down to face him on his level. "I'm Dr. Chambers, but you can call me Dr. Julia."

"You're a girl!"

"You're right! And I hear you're a pretty sharp boy. Want to hear my heartbeat through the stethoscope?"

He did. Smiling, Julia let him do a miniature exam on herself, allowing him to look in her ear and nose with the otoscope, listen to her heartbeat, and look down her throat. And all the while she was conscious of Ben sitting in the corner, watching her.

"You'd make a fine doctor someday," she told him, and he beamed. "Now I'm going to talk with you mother for a few minutes."

She asked Mrs. Locke about Avery's eating and sleeping habits, confirmed he had no bladder or bowel problems, and asked how he was doing in school.

Then she gave Avery a physical. She checked his eyesight and hearing, took his height and weight, had him write his name, and heard him count to twenty-five.

"Wonderful, Avery!" she said. "You're obviously a bright boy. Now, you know you're going to have to get some shots today, right?"

Concern clouded his face. "Yeah. That's what mom said. Do...do I hafta?"

"I'm afraid so. A little moment of pain is a lot better than getting some of these diseases. Would you like to sit on your mother's lap while I give them to you? Or would you rather be on the exam table?"

Avery, brave lad, elected to sit on the exam table while Julia administered polio, DTP, and Hepititus A shots.

Only one tear escaped him, and though his lower lip wobbled, he didn't cry.

"Wow!" exclaimed Julia after it was all over. "You mom was right when she said you were the bravest kid in your school! I think this deserves a prize." She pulled the basket of children's treats out of a drawer, and Avery's wobbly lip vanished like magic as he rooted among the little toys and stickers.

"That went well," Ben commented as Avery and his mother left the clinic. "You have a good touch with kids."

"I like kids. You're right in saying he's cute. He reminds me of Opie in *The Andy Griffith Show*."

Ben chuckled, a warm welcoming sound. Julia busied herself in writing up the report on Avery's exam because she didn't want to acknowledge just how much she liked Ben's laugh.

The day alternated between scheduled appointments and walk-ins. "...no where *near* as intense as in Portland," observed Julia. "I can actually sit down for lunch."

"We don't have the population you have in Portland," replied Ben, biting into a sandwich.

The walk-ins ranged from lacerations requiring stitches, to sprained ankles. The highlight of the afternoon, however, was Sandra Kepke, who like her twin sister Sara was showing signs of developing pre-eclampsia during the latter half of her pregnancy.

"Sandra, this is Dr. Julia Chambers," introduced Ben.

Sandra's eyes sparkled. "A woman doctor! You have no idea what a relief that is." She winked at Ben. "This guy's good, but there's some relief in knowing that the person looking at my private parts is *not* the jerky kid who pulled my hair in fourth grade."

Julia chuckled, liking the woman immediately. "I guess that's one of the *disadvantages* of having a home-town doctor," she said.

"Okay, give me the full range of problems," interspersed Ben.

It was clear that Sandra was used to this request. "Heartburn, hemorrhoids, swollen ankles, clumsiness, shortness of breath, low back pain, constipation, swollen veins...." She paused, and finished, "It's *hell* being a woman sometimes." Then she smiled. "Will I live?"

"Well, *you'll* live, and I'm going to make sure your baby does too." He hauled a blood pressure cuff out of a drawer and dropped it. "Damn. Julia, can you grab that? Let's check her blood pressure. And Sandra, I'll let Julia examine you, if you don't mind. Too hard for me to do from a sitting position."

"Sure," said Sandra. "Just leave the room and gimme a little privacy, will ya?"

When Ben had left the room, Julia took Sandra's blood pressure and frowned at the result—140/90. "Has Dr. Taylor told you the symptoms to watch for that indicate you might be developing pre-eclampsia?" she asked.

"Yes."

"Then you know that high blood pressure is one of the things to watch for. I measured 140 over 90—your chart says your last reading showed 120 over 70. I think we can safely say that you're at high risk."

Sandra sighed. "I know. And Sara lost her last baby due to this." She blinked rapidly. "Darn it, there I go again. It's these hormones, making me turn into a watering pot at the drop of a hat."

"Well, you have some concerns." *She wasn't the only one*, thought Julia. *Why couldn't Sandra have some other condition?* "But we'll do our best to get you through. Is this your urine sample?"

"Yes."

"I'll have Adele do a protein and sugar analysis." She delivered the lidded cup to the nurse practitioner, and returned to the room. "Ready for your exam?"

"Sure." Sandra lay down on the exam table, and Julia gently palpated the fetus, feeling for position and size. She listened to the heartbeat, measured Sandra's size, and monitored the number of fetal kicks.

"Seems a little smaller than I'd like," commented Julia. "But the heartbeat is strong, which is good. I see your weight is up twenty pounds in the last month—that's a large gain for a fairly short amount of time, and I don't think it's because you're eating too much. It's because you're retaining water."

"I know. Look at my ankles. And my hands. My face isn't normally shaped like a moon, either."

"Are you taking your prenatal vitamins?"

"Yes. Every day."

"Good. Okay, here's what I want you do to. Eliminate anything from your diet that has lots of salt and not much nutritional content. No potato chips, as few pre-packaged foods as possible. You need to eat a lot of meat, for protein, as well as lots of dark green leafy vegetables. Legumes, too—peas, beans, lentils. Cut down your coffee intake—"

"Why the sudden change in diet?"

"Because you're becoming anemic, meaning your blood is getting thin. Your body is supplying blood to your baby, and it often causes anemia in pregnancy. If you don't correct it now, you could miscarry."

Sandra sniffed. "I understand. I'll try to eat better."

"Good. If you have any bleeding, or any trouble with severe headaches or changes in your eyesight, come in immediately. *Immediately*, do you understand?"

Sandra's eyes widened with fear, and Julia cursed herself. *Don't scare the woman, idiot,* she thought.

"Why immediately?"

"Because those conditions always need to be checked out," Julia replied lightly. She didn't mention that those symptoms could be life-threatening. "Don't worry, Sandra—we'll get you through this."

"Can I—can I keep working?" asked Sandra.

Should have thought of that sooner, Julia thought. "What kind of job do you have?"

"I'm a secretary at the mill."

"Lots of sitting? No heavy lifting?"

"No."

"Then for now, yes. But if your condition grows into full-blown pre-eclampsia, then you'll have to be on bed-rest for the remainder of your pregnancy."

Sandra sniffed again and wiped her eyes. "Okay."

Julia gathered up the charts and files. "I'll leave you to get re-dressed. Stop at the front and make an appointment for next Monday."

She met Ben in the hallway, and asked to see him in her office. "Come into mine instead," he said. "It's hard to roll onto that carpet in your office in the wheelchair."

Gypsy was curled up on a dog bed in the corner of Ben's office. She lifted her head and blinked at Julia with sleepy eyes but didn't get up.

"What did you think of Sandra?" asked Ben.

"I'm worried." Julia seated herself opposite Ben's desk. "She has every sign of developing pre-eclampsia. I've advised her on dietary changes, and told her that she might have to quit her job and go on bed-rest if things worsen."

He nodded. "Both she and Sara—that's her twin

26

sister—have the same problems. Sandra's a month further along than Sara. I've already told them both that they may have to go stay in Moscow towards their 37th week so they can have facilities at Gritman Medical Center available. Gritman has an excellent neo-natal ICU too."

"Another high-risk maternity case," muttered Julia to herself. She felt cold fear champ her insides.

"What's that?"

"Oh, nothing." Julia lifted her head and gave Ben a bright smile. "It's just that I like Sandra. I'd hate to see anything happen to the baby."

"That's why I'll do everything I can to make sure it's born in Moscow, not here," he replied. "Jasper is not prepared for a toxemic birth, at least with much hope of a happy outcome." He gave her a decisive nod. "That's the one thing about being a GP—you have to learn your limitations."

*****

Julia got home just before dark. Her feet hurt from being on them most of the day, and she had a tension headache throbbing in her temples. She flipped lights on and felt the cat curl around her ankles. It was nice, she had to admit, to have someone—even a cat—to come home to.

The house was cold, and it took her fifteen minutes to get a fire going. Once the flames caught the wood, she sat back and watched the flicker through the isinglass windows for a few minutes, thinking.

You have to learn your limitations...

Pre-eclampsia.

Julia yanked the large bobby pins out of her hair and let the dark mass cascade past her waist while she rubbed tension from her scalp. Pre-eclampsia. Oh God, not again. Of all the cases to be socked with in some backwater rural facility, why did it have to be pre-eclampsia?

Well, she *had* learned her limitations. One thing was certain—when Sandra Kepke came back for her next appointment, she's make sure Ben was the one who saw her.

The cat jumped onto her lap and purred. "Who did you belong to before I moved here?" she asked rhetorically, scratching the animal under the chin. "I can't believe someone would abandon a pretty thing like you. Though I have to admit that if the people I saw today are any indication, Jasper is a nicer place than I would have given credit for."

It was true. She liked her coworkers. She liked her patients. So far so good.

She thought maybe she could get to like Jasper after all. "If I can wiggle out of taking on the pre-eclampsia cases," she told the cat, "I'll get along just fine. Maybe I'm glad I came here after all."

Until the next day. From the first, Julia knew it was going to be a rotten day.

Ben was gone again, called out to a case in some outlying district. Julia's first appointment was with a six-year-old boy. His mother had three children ranging in age from four to ten, and was pregnant with a fourth.

The children were well-groomed and polite. The mother was quiet and deferential. No problem.

The boy was returning for an ear checkup following a severe ear infection—otitis—a few weeks before. No problem.

"Looks like he had a pretty bad ear infection," said Julia, looking over the boy's file. "Well, John, I'm going to do something called a tympanogram on you today. Do you know what that is?"

"No, what?" asked the boy.

"Well, you know that inside your ear is a membrane called an eardrum, right?"

"Right."

"Well, the way an eardrum helps you hear is

that it vibrates back and forth, like this." Julia vibrated her hand. "That vibration translates into sound in your brain. Because you had that nasty ear infection awhile back, I need to test your eardrum."

"Will—will it hurt?"

"Not at all. See this? This little machine is called a tympanometer. It makes a quiet noise inside your ear. I can measure how much it gets your eardrum moving. Watch out though—it might tickle!"

John giggled as the instrument went into his ear. Julia turned it on and watched the scope record the readings. The tympanic membrane looked fine, but she detected a retraction of one ear drum.

"Well, John, you did great. Did it tickle a lot?"

"Yeah. Sort of."

Julia turned to the mother. "There's a little concern still with that one ear drum. I'd like to see him in another month or so."

"Okay."

"Also, I notice that John—or any of the children..." she added, flipping papers in the file, "...have not had their childhood vaccinations."

"That's right," Mrs. Doyle told Julia. "Nor will they."

Julia laid her pen down and looked at the woman. "And can you tell me why?"

"Because I don't believe in vaccinations."

Julia felt slow irritation start inside her. "So you don't believe in protecting your children?"

"I *am* protecting my children. I won't let foreign stuff be introduced into their systems. Besides, it's normal for children to get childhood illnesses like mumps and chicken pox. It builds up their resistance."

"Mrs. Doyle, you cannot build resistance to things like polio or Hepatitis A or diphtheria."

"Those diseases don't exist around here."

"They certainly *do* exist, but they're less

frequent because people have been vaccinated."

"See? Then I don't have to vaccinate *my* children because they won't get any of these illnesses."

Julia shook her head. "There are always dormant populations of diseases, waiting to strike unprotected people. I strongly urge you to let me vaccinate your children at least for polio, Mrs. Doyle."

"No."

Julie counted to ten so that the slow-building anger inside her wouldn't show. "Can I ask what your objections to vaccination are? Besides the introduction of foreign stuff into their systems?"

"Well, vaccinations cause autism."

"No, they don't. There are no clinical studies that show a link between autism and any vaccinations."

"That's what *you* say. But there have been lots and lots of children who have developed autism after getting shots."

"I'm not denying that autism is on the rise, but there's no cause and affect between autism and shots. It's like...well, broccoli. One hundred percent of people who eat broccoli will die, but that doesn't mean eating broccoli kills you. There's no cause and effect correlation between the two, just as there isn't between vaccinations and autism."

"You're *not* giving my children any shots."

"Mrs. Doyle, please—"

The quiet, deferential stance was dropped as Mrs. Doyle stood up and glared at Julia, her eyes narrowed. "Look, just because you're a big city doctor doesn't mean you know all the answers. You're harassing me about these shots, and I won't have it. I'm going home. Come on, kids."

The pregnant woman swept out of the office, muttering. Julia looked after her and saw Ben coming down the hall, evidently returning from his

30

call.

"What's up?" he asked, after Mrs. Doyle had swept past him in a huff.

Julia made a face. "You were right about some people objecting to vaccinations. She got touchy and left because I was trying to urge her to let her kids have the polio vaccine at least. I—I'm afraid I may not have handled it very well."

"I'm sure you did fine."

Julia shook her head. "And she's pregnant too. God, if she gets rubella that baby could be born deaf. And I'll bet you ten-to-one I'm the one on call when she goes into labor."

"You won't be, because I'll bet you ten-to-one she has the baby at home with a midwife."

Julia looked startled. "A home birth?"

"Of course." He shrugged. "Again, it's fairly common around here. We lose a few infants every year because of it. I don't like it, but there's not much we can do."

She shook her head. "It's a whole new world out here—Looks like you have an appointment now," she said, and gestured toward a woman following Lisa down the hallway toward an exam room.

He nodded. "Mary Lansing. See you later." He wheeled himself around and disappeared into the exam room.

Julia went into her office to write up the results of her last appointment. Within five minutes, however, there was a quiet buzz on her intercom. "Julia? Dr. Taylor wants to know if you can join him in Exam Room A."

"Be right there," she replied. Snatching up her stethoscope, she hurried to the room.

"Ah, here you are," said Ben congenially. Too congenially. Julia looked close and saw lines of tension around his eyes. "Mrs. Lansing, this is Dr. Julia Chambers, our new Resident. Julia, I thought you and Mrs. Lansing could become acquainted while I look in on a new patient."

He left the room and Julia stared after him, wondering what was up. There *were* no new patients at the moment, and she knew Ben knew that. Then she turned to offer her hand to Mrs. Lansing...and stalled.

The woman sported a black eye and several bruises along her left cheek. She also winced as Julia shook her hand, and the source of pain seemed to be her upper arm or shoulder. Her handshake was weak. Her shoulders were hunched. She looked to be in her late forties with watery blue eyes and brown hair that was graying.

Julia assumed a pleasant, bland expression. "It's nice to meet you, Mrs. Lansing. Are you here to have your eye treated?"

"Yes," the woman whispered. "I—I ran into a doorframe. Clumsy of me, I'm afraid."

"Oh, it happens to the best of us. Let me look at it." Julia probed carefully and felt around the eye socket. "Does this hurt? Or this? Good. It doesn't look like the eye socket is broken." She walked over and pressed the intercom. "Adele? Could you bring me an ice pack, please? Thanks." She turned back to Mrs. Lansing. "Applying cold will keep the swelling down. It also constricts the blood vessels and will slow internal bleeding, which is what causes the discoloration.—Thanks, Adele," she added, as the nurse handed her the ice pack.

Julia carefully laid the pack over the woman's eye. "You'll want to keep this on your eye for about ten minutes every two hours," she said. "Don't press on it; just let it rest over your eye. Do you have acetaminophen at home?"

"What's that?"

"Tylenol or one of the generic equivalents?"

"Um, I don't think so...I have aspirin..."

32

"Don't take aspirin. Aspirin is an anticoagulant, so the blood won't clot as well. You could end up with a bigger bruise." Julia rummaged in a drawer and pulled out a sample bottle of Tylenol. "Take this instead. It will also help with the pain. Now—what about your arm—what hurts?"

"My arm?" The woman's good eye widened in alarm. "My arm is fine."

"Let me see." She took Mrs. Lansing's right arm and gently palpated it from the elbow up to the shoulder as the woman winced in pain. "Can I have you remove your shirt, Mrs. Lansing? It's easier for me to see the muscle structure without it. Here, let me help."

As she expected, there were numerous bruises on the woman's chest and neck. Julia said nothing as she examined the arm. "Looks like some strained ligaments. If you rest it and try to minimize how much you lift or move your arm, the ligaments should heal up in a week or so. I'll help you get your shirt back on."

When the older woman had her clothing back in, Julia sat opposite her. "Why did he beat you up?" she asked gently.

Mrs. Lansing jumped. "B-beat me up? Who?"

"I don't know. You tell me. Was it your husband?"

The watery eyes blinked rapidly. "Y—yes."

"I figured it was. Now Mrs. Lansing, are you ready to leave and get into a shelter? I doubt there are any here locally, but I'm sure Moscow has some. You can't stay in the kind of environment you're in now."

"Leave? I can't leave Lenny."

"But nor can you stay. Do you have any minor children at home?"

"No, they're all grown and gone."

"And you're alone with someone who's giving

33

you black eyes and twisting your arm so hard that he's damaging the ligaments. Mrs. Lansing, I'm sure you understand that isn't safe, nor is it normal, to have a husband who beats you."

"I can't leave," the woman repeated.

"You're afraid, I know. Would you like me to call a shelter in Moscow right now? We can get you over there this afternoon, you wouldn't have to go back home at all—"

"No. I can't." Mrs. Lansing stood up. "I really can't. Th-thank you for your offer, Dr. Chambers, but I can't."

She yanked open the door and fled outside.

Second patient in a half-hour running away from me, Julia thought. She felt bleak that she couldn't penetrate Mary Lansing's stubborn—or fearful—refusal for help.

"So what's the situation?" asked Ben, coming around the corner from his office.

Julia turned and crossed her arms on her chest. "Why did you dump her on me with no warning?"

"I had no way to prepare you. She wasn't about to open up to me, and I figured she might talk to another woman rather than to a man. Was I right?"

"Oh yes." Julia slumped against the wall and ran a hand over her hair. "Classic case of spousal abuse. Yanks her arms behind her back so hard her ligaments are strained. Blackens her eye. The bastard. Yet she's heading back to him right now."

Ben sighed. "I've seen her quite a few times over the last year. Lenny Lansing has always had a temper, but he never seemed to take it out on Mary until their last kid left home. Beating up on Mary seems to be his newest hobby. She always explains things away, though—ran into a doorframe, tripped and fell, that kind of thing."

"We can't even call Child Protective Services on this."

"No." Ben gave her a grim smile. "Makes me wish there was a Wife Protective Services around."

"What do you know about Lenny Lansing? Besides the fact that he has a temper."

Ben stroked his chin. "Hmmm—well, he works at the mill. He's a straight-shooter—works hard, doesn't drink much. Seems to be well-enough liked by the boys he works with."

"And this thing—this beating up on his wife—is fairly recent?"

"Fairly. For the last year or so."

"Could he be on drugs?"

Ben sat quiet a moment, thinking. "Could be. There's a methamphetamine problem in this county, and maybe he got caught up."

"Maybe. Either way, I'm going to work on Mary Lansing whenever I can—maybe stop in and see her when I know Lenny won't be home, just to let her know she can come to me if she needs help."

"That's decent of you, Julia."

"Decent, nothing." Julia clenched her fists. "It blows me away when women stay with men like that. I tried to urge her to go to a shelter, but she wouldn't leave her husband."

"Hey, remember the old adage about doctors having to remain detached and unemotional about their patients? Here's an example. Help her all you can, but don't take Mary on as a personal triumph or failure."

"It's hard, not getting personally involved." *You have no idea how hard,* she thought. It could be argued that she was here *because* of a case in which she got personally involved.

"But it's necessary to keep sane in this business."

"That doesn't mean I'm going to stop trying to convince her to leave him."

"Nor should you stop. I'm just saying that Mary

will have to make her own decisions, for good or bad, and while you may be able to influence her, you can't take Mary on as a personal cause."

Julia turned away, still clenching her fists. "Wrenched her arm backwards, blackened her eye..." she muttered.

"Ben!" yelled Lisa from the reception area. "Anaphylactic shock!"

Startled, both Julia and Ben jerked around. Julia took off running, Ben wheeled his chair to the front as quickly as he could.

A man stood panting in the reception room. He had a wild, scruffy look to him, with unkempt beard and hollow cheeks. If Julia had met him in a dark alley, she'd be inclined to run screaming in the other direction.

But frank terror was on his face for the small, unconscious girl he held in his arms. "Bee sting!" he gasped.

Julia nodded and snapped, "Follow me! Ben, Room A."

Ben was already rolling his chair in that direction. By the time Julia and the man followed, he had pulled a syringe of epinephrine from a cabinet.

Julia had the man lay the child on the exam table. She looked to be about five, and Julia estimated her weight at thirty-five pounds. Her face and hands were swollen, and she had hives on her skin. Her breathing was labored, shallow, and decreasing. "Where was the sting?" she asked the man.

"On the side of her neck."

Bad location. "Do you want to intubate, Ben?"

"No. Not yet. She's still breathing, though it's shallow. Let's see how she responds to the sub-Q." He injected the child with epinephrine sub-cutaneously, possibly the most effective remedy to severe shock. "Check her blood pressure."

Julia yanked the monitor over and fastened the cuff around the slim arm. The moments passed as Ben watched her for reaction to the epinephrine and Julia monitored the blood pressure. "90 over 60," she said, and pulled off the ear pieces.

"Low. The Benadryl is in that cabinet over there—we'll give it to her IM." He stared at the child a moment. "Wait—her breathing is improving—check the pressure again."

Julia turned back with a Benadryl syringe in her hand. She dropped the syringe on the counter in order to puff up the blood pressure cuff on the child's arm again. She listened to the heartbeat and a smile lit her face. "110 over 72. She's responding."

"Give her the Benadryl anyway. With a reaction this severe, I don't want to take any chances."

Julia injected the child intramuscularly. As she did so, the girl gave a gasp and began crying.

It sounded like music.

Behind them the man whispered "Jessie!" and moved towards her. Julia had forgotten about him. "She'll be all right now," she said, and laid a comforting hand on his arm. "Just a bad scare."

The girl opened her eyes and looked frightened at the unfamiliar surroundings and faces. "Daddy?"

"I'm here, baby." He looked at Ben. "Can I hold her?"

"You bet." He moved his chair out of the way.

The man gathered the little girl into his arms, heedless of the blood pressure cuff still dangling. "Hush, baby, hush. It's all right, daddy's here."

Tears pricked Julia's eyes. He looked so shabby, yet the tenderness he showed the girl spoke for itself. She could only imagine the terror the man had gone through, watching his daughter suffer such a severe reaction to a simple bee sting.

"She gonna be okay?" the man asked, blinking

rapidly.

"Yes." Julia took a discrete sniff and gently removed the blood pressure cuff. "You need to be equipped with a bee sting kit at all times to use in case she has another sting. We'll show you how to use it."

"What did you give her?" the man asked. "It worked so fast!"

"Epinephrine," Ben said. He smiled. "One of the miracles of the medical world, if you ask me. It acts by constricting blood vessels, which increases blood pressure. It also widens the airways." He sobered. "I have to tell you this, though—if you hadn't gotten her here when you did, she might have died from suffocation. Getting stung in the neck meant that her airway was nearly swelled shut. You did good, Clem."

The man nodded and closed his eyes while he held the girl tight.

"Ben, let's go up front and start filling in the paperwork," Julia said quietly. "Let's give him a chance to calm down."

Chapter Three

Julia got home just before dark. As before, she flipped lights on and felt the cat curl around her ankles. As before, she thought how nice it was to have someone—even a cat—to come home to. She sat down and let the cat jump into her lap.

"Well, cat, I'm changing my mind. It looks like Jasper is a backwards, yokel-infested backwater after all."

The cat purred and rubbed her neck into Julia's fingers.

"We got a wife beater. We got someone who thinks vaccinating her kids will kill them." She sighed. "But we also got the scruffiest, grungiest-looking man I've ever seen who looked like the world's best daddy. Go figure."

She heard a noise outside her door and lifted her head, wary. Jasper might not be Portland, but that didn't mean there couldn't be home invasions. She lifted the cat off her lap, tiptoed to the door, and quietly twisted the deadbolt before peeking through the window.

Ben was on the walkway, struggling to pick up something he'd dropped and cursing softly. Julia smiled and relaxed.

She unlocked the door and leaned against the door frame, watching.

"It's a good thing you're not condemned to be in that chair for a lifetime," she told him. "You couldn't cope."

He uttered another curse word. "Can you give

me a hand here? I dropped some stuff and I can't seem to pick it up."

A delectable smell wafted to her nose. "Is that pizza I smell?"

"It is." He lifted a bag from his lap to reveal a box balanced on his knees. "I was starving, and figured you might be too."

"Where's the pizza place in this town? I didn't know there was one." Julia stepped outside and picked up the bag he'd dropped.

"Over on First Street. They make a pretty good pizza, all things considered."

"Here, let me put all this inside before I help you up that step." Julia grabbed his other bag as well as the pizza box and carried them inside before coming out to hoist Ben's chair over that step. "If you make a habit of visiting, I'm going to lay a piece of plywood over this step to make a ramp."

"You may not need to bother." Ben grunted a bit as the chair came down heavily over the threshold. "I talked to my orthopedic surgeon this afternoon, and he says that I'm healing up so fast that I may be out of this thing sooner than I thought. Maybe by Friday."

"Yeah? That's great! Then you won't be dropping blood pressure cuffs everywhere."

"I see you got the hang of the woodstove." He nodded towards where the flames showed merrily.

"Yes, and quite a difference it makes, too." She walked back in the kitchen and flipped open the pizza box. "Mmmmm... pepperoni, sausage, and mushrooms. Perfect."

"There's parmesan garlic bread and root beer too."

"Quite a spread. So, to what do I owe this honor?"

"Oh, call it a welcome-to-Jasper feast. And for a day's work well done."

40

Julia started pulling plates from a cabinet. She handed Ben some glasses, and he poured the root beer.

He lifted his beverage in a toast. "To saving lives. We hauled that kid back from death's door, always a nice feeling."

Julia toasted him back, then distributed some pizza onto the plates. "I won't argue with you there. It *was* a nice feeling, especially after a pretty crappy day."

"Crappy? How?"

"Patients walking out on me left and right. I managed to insult Mrs. Doyle about the vaccinations, and then Mary Lansing fled the office without letting me help her."

"Hey, you win some, you lose some. You won with Jessie, that's for sure. You have a cool head in an emergency."

Julia felt a chill run through her. "Depends on the emergency," she muttered. "So who *was* that guy, anyway?" she added. "The girl's father? He looked...well, wild. Scary."

"That's Clem Parker. Lost his wife to cancer a couple years ago, sadly. He dotes on his little girl, as you can see."

"It brought tears to my eyes, watching him with her."

"Yeah, Clem's quite a guy." Ben chewed some garlic bread thoughtfully. "Something of a hermit. Holds a mining claim about five miles out of town. He also mans the fire tower for a couple months in the summer."

"What about Jessie? Does she go with him?"

"Oh you bet. They're inseparable."

"What grade is she in?"

"She's homeschooled."

Startled, Julia stared at him. "You're kidding! How can...I mean, surely he can't teach her...oh, that poor kid!"

Ben grinned. "He looks like a fourth-grade dropout, doesn't he?"

"Yes."

"He has a master's degree in geology from the University of Idaho, and an additional bachelor's degree in engineering." His smile widened. "Not to mention he's an author. He's published three layman's books on the geology of the region as well as a novel. Believe me; he's *well* qualified to teach her."

Stunned at the revelation of the man who would have sent her running from a dark alley, Julia shook her head. "What a place of contrasts this is."

"I agree. It's a place I find fascinating, despite having grown up here."

"You never get bored or find yourself too limited?"

"Not often. I love hiking and fishing and swimming, and this place has opportunities for all three in abundance."

"Swimming? Is there a community pool?"

"No, there's Lake Percheron."

"You swim in *a lake?*"

"Sure. Clean water, and it's got some of the nicest beaches around. I'll show you some time. What about you? What do you like to do in your off-time?"

She shrugged. "Read. Shop. Sew. Not that I've had much time for any of those since being in med school, of course."

"You like to *sew?*"

She raised her eyebrows. "Yes. Why do you find that so astonishing?"

"I've always admired women who can sew. Were you keeping that a secret? It surprises me that a city girl would enjoy something as wholesome as sewing."

"Wholesome?" Julia swallowed a bite. "Do you think that just because I grew up in the city, that I'm full of vile habits or something?"

"Nope. But I find you fascinating—full of surprises and secrets." His eyes twinkled.

Julia couldn't help smiling. "Did you bring this pizza over to bribe me into revealing all the sordid secrets of my past?"

"Maybe. Just wanted to get to know you better, that's all."

"Well, don't. I'm not interested in...well, getting known better. I'm a temporary Resident here and I'll be gone inside three months, back to the city where I'm most comfortable."

"I see. Tell me—do you ever let your hair down?"

She blinked at the change in subject. "My hair? Do you mean figuratively or literally?"

"Literally. It looks long and beautiful. Ever let it down?"

"I don't see how that concerns you. Tell me, Dr. Taylor, do you compliment all the Residents who work at the clinic?"

"Nope. Just the pretty ones. And the available ones."

She pulled herself back. "Well, forget it. I'm not available."

"Why not? Boyfriend back in Portland?"

"No. But I have my reasons." She turned her back toward him. "And no, I won't discuss what they are."

"Hmm. We'll see about that. In the meantime, I'll continue to dream about that hair."

She glared at him over her shoulder. "Maybe I'm not so eager to have you out of that chair after all."

"Oh, you're safe for awhile. I might be out of the chair soon, but I have a fair bit of rehabilitative physical therapy to go through."

"In Moscow?"

"Yes."

Julia paused, conflicted. She wanted to keep Ben at arm's length. On the other hand... how could she have him stay on top of the pre-eclampsia case if he were in Moscow?

"Why so quiet all of a sudden?"

She told him the truth...or at least part of it. "I don't want to encourage you toward any—er—inappropriate interest, Ben. But I'll also confess that I have certain knack for physical therapy. I loved the rotation I did in that field, so if you need help with your therapy..."

"Gosh, I'm flattered."

"Don't be. You'll be a patient, then—and remember what you've warned me about not getting personally involved with my patients?"

"I guess I'll take my chances then. And yes, thanks, I'd be pleased to have you do the physical therapy. It'll beat going to Moscow two or three times a week." He finished his food and pushed back from the table. "And on that encouraging note, I'm going home and hit the hay. Keep the pizza, unless you want to bring the cold leftovers to work tomorrow for lunch."

Julia helped Ben down the step, and locked the door behind him. Then she leaned against the door and took a deep breath. Having to fight off an interest from her boss wasn't something she anticipated...or wished for.

Maybe.

Darn it, she liked Ben. He seemed like a talented, compassionate doctor. He was good-looking in a non-flashy way. And he had a wonderful bedside manner.

Unlike Alex, who was a brilliant internist, was gorgeous, and had a feeling of superiority that permeated everything he did. Alex wouldn't be caught dead in a little backwater place like Jasper.

General practitioner work didn't appeal to someone of Alex's caliber.

Nor, apparently, did she.

Sighing, she went about closing down the house. She packed the woodstove with logs and turned down the damper so the heat would last through the night, then clicked off the lights. In the bathroom, she took the pins out of her hair and let the mass tumble free, thinking about Ben's comment. She shivered with...something.

Interest?

Maybe.

****

Ben went into Moscow on Friday for an appointment with his orthopedic surgeon, leaving Julia in charge of the clinic. Fortunately it was slow—slow enough that Julia had time to run to Betty's Café for some coffee. She had to admit that Betty made wonderful coffee.

She met Sara Johanson, whose twin sister Sandra she had met earlier. Julia's stomach clenched with nerves when Sara walked in. However, she introduced herself and greeted her warmly. "Whew! You guys *are* identical. How will I tell you apart?"

"Well, Sandra's a month farther a long than I am. That'll work until we have our babies."

As with Sandra, Julia liked Sara right away...which only made it harder for Julia.

"Your blood pressure is up," said Julia. She took the pieces from her ear and unwrapped the cuff from Sara's arm. "Are you watching your salt intake?"

"Yes, closely, especially since you warned Sandra about that on Friday."

"You're also edemic."

"Meaning...?"

"Meaning your hands and ankles are puffy because you're retaining water. Your face too."

45

"Tell me about it." Sara looked at her protruding belly. "I—I lost our last baby. My husband Gus and I are desperate to start a family." She sniffed and swiped at her nose, and Julia reached over and plucked a tissue from a box for her. "Thanks. Ben says that around my 37th week, I should go stay in Moscow so I can be near the hospital in…in case something happens."

"A wise precaution." *And a wonderful idea*, Julia thought. "Why don't you lie down and let me see how the baby's growing."

Sara lay on the exam table, and Julia took a tape measure and measured the dome of Sara's belly. Then she gently palpated the abdomen.

"How the baby doing?" asked Sara.

"Smaller than I like for this stage of your pregnancy. But the heartbeat is strong. You're carrying a fighter. Do you know if it's a boy or a girl?"

"No, we wanted to be surprised." A wan smile cracked Sara's face. "Ben knows, of course, from the ultrasound, but we've forbidden him to tell us. I keep dreaming about a boy, though."

"Have you chosen names?"

"Samuel Robert for a boy. Mary Elaine for a girl."

"Beautiful." She offered her hand, and Sara clasped it to help sit up. "Well, so far so good. As long as you continue watching your diet, we'll keep monitoring you and let you know when you should go to Moscow. I'll let you get dressed now. Stop by the receptionist's desk on your way out to schedule your next appointment."

Julia had to resist the urge to shove poor Sara out the door. She was ashamed of her reaction. She was a doctor, a professional, and someone as pleasant and clearly in need of medical care as Sara didn't need Julia to fall apart on her.

The rest of the day was slow. A boy with a broken arm from falling off his skateboard. An elderly woman for her flu shot. A strapping man who blushed as Julia conducted a DOT physical on him for his truck driver's exam.

Half an hour before the clinic closed for the weekend, Ben walked in, leaning heavily on a cane. But he *walked* in.

"Look at you!" said Lisa.

Adele turned around from a file she was reading. "You're on your feet!" she exclaimed.

Hearing the voices, Julia stepped into the receptionists' office. "Wow! You're out of the wheelchair!"

He grinned all around, but his eyes lingered a moment on Julia. "It's a bit painful," he admitted, "but it feels good to stand up again!"

Julia didn't say anything as the two other women fluttered around him. Upright, Ben topped her by four or five inches. His body had no doubt lost some muscle tone during his stint in the wheelchair, but she became aware of his breadth of chest and impressive physique.

He was gorgeous.

Yikes.

And she had offered to help him with his physical therapy! The thought of laying her hands on his legs and hips—purely for medicinal purposes, of course, to help him recover his strength and range of motion—suddenly seemed disturbing and intimate.

"How have things been here today?" he asked her.

"Fine. Quieter than usual. I met Sara Johanson. She came in for her weekly checkup. She's definitely pre-eclamptic. Her blood pressure is high, and the baby's growth isn't as advanced as I'd like." Julia pointed out portions of Sara's file and avoided looking directly at Ben. "You had made a notation that she might need to go to Gritman Medical Center in Moscow when she hits 37 weeks."

"That's right." He drew close and looked over her shoulder at Sara's chart while Julia froze and tried not to act too disturbed at his proximity. "She looks as good as can be expected at this stage."

Julia closed the file and moved to place the folder in Lisa's in-box. "At what week of pregnancy did she lose the last baby?"

"38 weeks. It was rough on her and her husband Gus. That's why I'm not taking any chances with this baby—I want Sara safely in Moscow before there's any chance of premature labor."

"Me too," muttered Julia. "But why are you waiting until 37 weeks to send her to Moscow?"

Ben looked at her. "What do you mean?"

"I mean, if she lost her last baby at 38 weeks, wouldn't it be advisable to send her earlier? I'm sure her insurance company would cover that, with her history." Julia didn't mention her own desire to have the woman out of town.

"You may have a point there, Julia. We can discuss it with Sara as well."

"I'm heading home, guys," said Lisa. She shrugged on her coat. "I promised John I'd make a meatloaf for dinner, and it takes awhile to cook."

"Yeah, it's quittin' time," said Adele. "Been quiet here while you were gone, Ben, except for Jim Sanders who broke his arm falling off his skateboard. With luck it'll stay quiet all weekend long. G'night."

Within minutes both women were gone, and Julia was alone with Ben.

"How does the leg feel?" she asked.

He sat down heavily and stretched it in front of him, flexing the foot and wincing. "Sore. I'm on pain meds for about a week, but nothing serious. I also

48

had my first session of PT. Hurt like hell." He grinned at her. "Does your offer still stand?"

"Maybe. It depends on whether or not you'll behave yourself." She couldn't help but smile back.

Big mistake. Attraction sprang up between them. Julia's smile dropped and she turned away.

"Julia," said Ben from behind her. "Don't turn away from me."

"Stop it, Ben. I don't want there to be anything between us."

"Why not?"

"I just don't."

"That's not a good enough reason."

"Ben, I don't owe you any reason at all. I don't want any sort of personal relationship with you. Deal with it." She walked around the room doing some purposeless tidying up.

"What are you afraid of?" he asked softly.

Startled, Julie turned and stared at him. "What?"

"You're running away from something. Otherwise there's no logical reason to deny the fact that you're as attracted to me just as much as I am to you."

She turned away. "That's none of your business. It's time to go home. Do you need help with anything?"

"No. Though it would serve you right if I said yes." He stood up and limped toward the hallway and his office. "Good night, Julia. Don't forget your beeper and cell phone. Be sure to keep them on you at all times."

****

...there is no logical reason to deny the fact that you're as attracted to me just as much as I am to you...

"He's far too perceptive," Julia told the cat as she gave him some more cat chow. She sat down and stroked the animal while he crunched up the food. "I suppose I'll have to give him some better reason than a vague 'none of your business' to put him off. Right?"

The cat ignored her while he satisfied his hunger. Julie wrapped her arms around her knees while she idly watched at the cat.

"I gotta get over this feeling of worthlessness," she muttered. Alex's desertion during her time of need still galled. It had been six months since the incident, and his departing words still stung. *You lost your head; you'll never make a decent doctor, that's why you're not suited to be anything better than a GP...*

Without realizing it, her fists clenched. Specialists often didn't understand how in-depth and demanding GP work was. And you'd never find a GP who had a snobby attitude problem, either...unlike specialists, who sometimes acted like they walked on water. Like Alex.

Sometimes Julia wondered what Alex ever saw in her. If he was so convinced that being a GP was...well, *demeaning*...then she wondered why the hell he ever became engaged to her to begin with.

In retrospect, she suspected her looks had something to do with it. No doubt it was a boost to Alex's ego to have a beautiful woman on his arm.

Julia knew she was beautiful. She also knew she could take no credit for it, so it didn't affect her ego one way or the other... except it attracted attention from men. Sometimes that was good, and sometimes not.

She wondered what category Ben fell into.

If Julia secretly hoped for a reason for Ben to drop by that Friday night, she was disappointed. As a result she rattled around the house, unable to settle with anything, and annoyed with herself for the vague longing she felt to see Ben again outside of the office.

She was up bright and early Saturday morning and ready to explore. She wanted to go to Moscow and see the town, feeling the need to immerse herself in, if not a city, at least a vibrant and active town. She could do some shopping, purchase some things to make her house more home-like, and see something of the countryside on her way to and fro.

The sun was shining, and for the first time Julia was able to see some of the beauty in the landscape that Ben had boasted about. The terrain alternated between heavy coniferous forests with tangles of underbrush, and wide prairie that had been plowed last fall and was now wet and muddy with the spring thaw. Forest and prairie. Forest and prairie. Green and brown. She drove over rolling hills, but it only took a quick glance in her rear-view mirror to see the beginnings of the Rocky Mountains thrusting up to the east. Jasper was truly in the foothills of these mighty peaks.

The ratio changed in favor of prairie over forest as she headed west. Moscow was a bustling little place. It had a vibrant, small-town charm, fueled by the economy of the University of Idaho. Julia wandered around the downtown, poking into bookstores and knickknack shops. Then she found her way to some large, modern stores on a newly-built complex on the outskirts of town. Here she purchased some items to make her rental house cozier.

She was standing before a Chinese restaurant, looking at the menu posted near the door, when she heard someone call her name. "Dr. Chambers?"

She turned and saw one of the pregnant twins from Jasper, but couldn't decide if it was Sandra or Sara.

"Hi!" Julia said brightly to hide her confusion. "Out for a day of shopping like me?"

"Yes. I'm Sandra, by the way."

Julia made a face. "Am I that obvious?"

"No, we're used to it. People mix us up all the time. Going in for lunch?"

"Yes."

"Mind if I join you?"

"Are you kidding?" Julia grinned. "I'd love it!" She glanced around. "You here by yourself?"

"Yes. My husband was working, and Sara had some stuff to do."

"Where does your husband work?"

"In Jasper. He's a sheriff."

Over mu-shu pork, Julia asked how Sandra was feeling. But Sandra waved her hand.

"This isn't a doctor's appointment. I'm doing fine. I'd rather talk about you. How do you like it in Jasper?"

"Well..."

Sandra gave her a cheeky smile. "A little slow, isn't it?"

"Yes," Julia confessed. "A lot different than Portland, that's for sure. I'm...I'm sure I'll get used to it, though."

"Maybe you will, maybe you won't. How long are you staying?"

"I have six months left of my residency, so I'll be here half of that. My resident hospital in Portland, ah, thought it best if I round out my training in a smaller, more rural facility. They said I'd be faced with more challenges here than if I stayed in a better equipped place like Portland." She blew out a breath. "So far I'd say they're right." She wasn't about to tell Sandra *why* the Portland hospital had sent her here.

"Well, as I said before, I'm delighted to have a woman doctor available," said Sandra.

"It's pretty obvious that Ben needed help, too," said Julia. "I'm surprised he was able to handle the clinic on his own in that wheelchair."

"InstaDoc helped a lot, especially at first," said Sandra. "But he couldn't be here all the time. There are other clinics that need him. I have a feeling Ben is quite pleased to have you here." Sandra cocked her head and assessed Julia's face. "*Quite* pleased."

Her meaning was obvious. Julia felt her cheeks flush. "Now Sandra, there's nothing like that..."

"Well, maybe there should be. He's quite a catch."

"I'm not here to catch anything, or be caught."

"Why not?"

Julia forced a laugh. "Why the sudden interest in match-making?"

"When you're a happily-married woman, you have a tendency to want to see everyone *else* happily married."

"Whoa!" Julia held up her hands, palms out. "Stop! I've just *met* the man, and you're already marrying us!"

Sandra chuckled. "Sorry. I get single-minded sometimes. But Ben's a great guy."

"So why isn't he married, then?" Julia kept her voice casual.

"Don't know." Sandra shrugged. "He was popular enough with the girls in high school. Then he disappeared and left town at eighteen. He was one of the few of us to leave and go to college. Then old Doc Anderson talked him into medical school with the promise that we'd all band together to pay for it...which became quite the event here in town. We held bake sales and car washes to pay for tuition. Ben did his part by living as frugally as he could while in Los Angeles."

Julia shook her head. "That amazes me, that a town this small could unify on something like that."

"It wasn't just the town, it was the whole county. Then the news media picked it up, and it got broadcast across the country, and we had money pouring in for awhile. We socked it all away towards his schooling."

"Wait a minute..." Julia's eyes unfocused as she thought back. "I seem to recall something like that hitting the national news a number of years ago, about how a town had banded together to put one of its own through medical school so he could become the town doctor...don't tell me that was here!"

"It was." Sandra beamed with pride. "It was a great time in our town's history, too. We had news wagons here nearly every month, interviewing people and talking with Doc Anderson. The library has all the news clippings and articles stored in a notebook if you ever want to read about it. The bank set up a fund, and any money that came in went straight into the bank. There's still money left over, I believe, that Ben uses when he needs stuff for the clinic. The ultrasound machine, for instance, so now no one has to go to Moscow for an ultrasound." She patted her large belly.

"Unbelievable. What about his family—did they help?"

Sandra's expression dropped. "He doesn't have any family, no brothers or sisters. His mother died when he was in college—I think her cancer is what spurred him to consider medicine—and afterward his dad left and moved to Phoenix. He died two years ago in a car accident."

"God, how sad."

"Yes. I liked his folks a lot, too."

The women were thoughtful for a moment.

"So anyway," Sandra resumed, "I think the reason Ben is still single is that he's just been too busy. He's only been in charge of the clinic for a couple of years, though he worked here for Dr. Anderson for a couple of years before that. Most of the girls he went to school with were married by the time he came back, and Jasper isn't exactly a hotbed of single women anyway." Sandra's eyes twinkled. "Until *you* showed up."

"Sandra..."

"Oh, c'mon, Dr. Chambers—"

Julia groaned. "Julia, please. I can't stand being called 'Dr. Chambers' by someone my own age who is eating fried rice with me."

"Julia, then. Now...why aren't *you* married?"

Julia nearly choked on her broccoli beef. "What?"

"Why aren't you married? You're gorgeous, Julia, and obviously smart. Why hasn't someone snapped you up years ago?"

Julia kept her eyes on her plate as she pushed her food around. She shrugged her shoulders. "No time either, I guess."

"Not good enough." Sandra chewed some rice. "Try another excuse."

"Persistent, aren't you?" Julia tried to be irritated, but couldn't. There was something so friendly about Sandra. And Julia needed a friend.

"Maybe. Or curious. Someone toss you over?"

"Yes." The moment the word left her lips, Julia wished she could take it back.

"That happens. Well, now you're here and can console yourself with a handsome man like Ben."

"Console, nothing. I'm still trying to deal with it."

"Ouch. Sorry. I hadn't realized it still stung."

"It didn't happen all that long ago."

"What was his name?"

"Alex."

"Was he a doctor?"

"Yes. Listen, Sandra, I really don't want to talk about it..."

"Hey, if you're worried that I'll gossip all over town, rest assured. I'm very good at keeping secrets."

She grinned. "Even from Sara."

But Julia was even better at keeping secrets, especially from pre-eclamptic patients whose friendship was an attractive lure for her. "Let's just say that he thought he was too good for me," she said. "He's an internist—someone who specializes in diseases of the internal organs," she added when she saw that Sandra didn't understand the term. "One thing you learn in med school is that specialists often look down at generalists. Alex always thought I was copping out by wanting to be a general practitioner."

"If he was such a snob, why did he go out with you at all?"

"Well..." Julia looked down at her plate.

And Sandra, with deadly feminine precision, picked it right up. "It was because of your looks, wasn't it?"

"Yes." Julia felt tears well up, and forced them back.

"Hey." Sandra reached over and patted Julia's hand. "Sounds like you did the right thing, dumping him."

"Well, *he* dumped *me*. Naturally that stings more than the reverse."

"The bastard."

The waiter came and dropped the lunch tickets on the table, and Julia realized that she and Sandra had lingered quite awhile. "Guess we ought to let them seat some other customers," she said. "Let me pay for this. My treat."

"Hmmph. Then why don't you come to dinner at our place next time you have a free night? You can meet my husband."

Warmth blossomed inside Julia. She realized how lonely she'd been for girlfriends. "That sounds great!"

They made arrangements, and parted with a

hug. Julia lingered for a moment outside the restaurant, watching Sandra walk down the street with waddling steps. Then she turned with a smile to get into her car. Maybe Jasper wouldn't be so bad after all.

Chapter Four

Five miles from Jasper, her cell phone rang. She fumbled to pull the phone out of her purse. "Hello?"

"It's Ben," he said.

Julia didn't want to admit how much her heart jumped at hearing his voice. "Hi. What's up?"

"Where are you?"

"About five miles outside of town, heading back from Moscow."

"Good. Meet me at the clinic. If you can avoid it, don't stop at home first. We have an emergency, and we'll have to drive to get there."

Julia didn't waste time in unnecessarily questions. "Be there in five minutes," she said. She hung up and stepped on the car's accelerator.

Ben was just coming out of the clinic with an enormous duffel bag, no doubt stuffed with medical supplies. He hardly let her pause, but limped over to the passenger side. "You can drive," he said. "I'm still not very fast."

"Which way?"

"East on this road, turn left when I tell you."

Julia swung the car onto the main road through town and headed east. After three blocks Ben said, "Turn left here. Keep going straight for about ten miles. I'll tell you where to go from there."

Julia followed his directions, and within moments were speeding out of town.

Ben leaned his head back. "First, thank you for not peppering me with questions, but just following directions. I won't try to order you around too much,

58

except when the occasion warrants."

"I like to think that's part of my medical training," Julia replied, her eyes on the road as she banked a curve. "So what's up?"

"Chain saw accident."

She winced. "Why didn't they drive in?"

"No car."

She threw him a startled glance. "And they live way out here? How do they get to town?"

"A few times a year they hitch a ride in with someone and buy supplies. But no one was available to take him into the clinic, so I figured it would go quicker for us to go out there."

"Well, at least they have a phone."

"Yes. At least there's that."

"So...did he amputate something?" Julia tried to keep her voice casual. Only once before, while doing an ER rotation, had she come across an accidental amputation... and it wasn't pretty.

"No. It's his left forearm. It wasn't severed, but his wife says there's extensive muscular damage and possible some nerve damage. I figure about all we can do is tie him together as best we can and transport him to Moscow."

"What about a Medivac?"

"We can get a helicopter down in the clinic parking lot, but not out here." He gestured out the window. "Too forested."

It was indeed. Julia had been too focused to pay much attention to the landscape, but she glanced around and realized that the conifers were thick and dense, with shafts of sun piercing to the forest floor and little undergrowth. "Wow. Pretty primeval. This kind of stuff could give you the willies at night, I imagine." Though it was the vision of what she might find at their destination that was giving her the willies, not the forest.

"I'll have to take you camping some time," he

replied. "You'd change your mind in a hurry. It's beautiful."

Within fifteen minutes, Ben directed her onto a rutted dirt road, and they bumped up as fast as they could. Julie stopped the car and jerked on the parking brake before a ramshackle cabin. A dirt yard was littered with rusted out cars, old bicycles, empty sacks of grain, and other detritus. A cow looked at them from a nearby pasture, chickens scratched among the garbage, and a horse lifted its head and whinnied.

Near a tree stump a chainsaw lay, sitting among a pool of bloody dirt.

A woman clad in a shapeless dress burst from the house. "Ben—Ben—thank God you're here—he's bleeding pretty heavily."

Ben hobbled as quickly as he could with his cane while Julie swung in behind him with the bag of medical supplies.

The inside of the cabin was rustic but surprisingly clean, considering the mess outside. A middle-aged man in overalls and work boots sat at the kitchen table, with his left arm swathed in bloody cloths and propped on a pile of small boards on the table. His face was pale and shiny with sweat.

"I've done what you said and elevated his arm," explained the woman breathlessly.

"Incipient shock," murmured Ben to Julia.

She saw the bluish lips, the clammy appearance, and suspected Ben was right. "He needs to lie down," she said. "Elevate the feet, cover him with a blanket."

"Who's that?" the man barked, glaring at Julia. Whatever his symptoms of shock were, it had not yet resulted in confused behavior.

"This is Dr. Julia Chambers," said Ben. "Julia, this is Jake and Mabel Smothers. So Jake, I hear you had a little run-in with your chain saw."

"Stupid bother over nothing," Jake muttered.

"It's *not* nothing," Mabel interposed. She looked pale herself, Julia noted. "You really should go to the hospital."

"Don't need no hospital, Mabel, I *told* you."

"Now Jake, don't start on Mabel," said Ben mildly as he felt Jake's pulse on his uninjured arm. "She's just trying to help. First things first, though: are you cold?"

"A little, maybe."

"You're starting to suffer from shock. Mabel, fetch him a blanket, will you? And Jake, I want you to lie down on the floor. Julia, grab those pillows from the couch. That's it, Jake. Head on this pillow, feet on those..."

"I feel stupid doing this..." Jake muttered.

"You'll feel stupider if you faint," replied Ben. "Any breathing problems? No? Good. Now when is the last time you had a tetanus shot?"

"It's been awhile," admitted Jake.

"Then you'll need one. Julia—"

Julia had anticipated this, and handed him a syringe the moment he turned around.

"Okay, this'll keep you from getting lockjaw," said Ben, as he injected the tetanus shot in Jake's right arm. "Now let's see what you've done to yourself."

He donned latex examination gloves that Julia handed him and began unwrapping the bloody cloths from Jake's left forearm. Julia stood with a packet of sterile gauze in her gloved hands. The moment the cloths fell away, the arm spurted blood. Ben applied pressure to the brachial artery while pressing on the wound with the gauze.

"Raney clips will tamponate the bleeding," said Julia, kneeling beside Jake. "As long as the edges are defined."

He nodded. "Grab some, will you? They're

somewhere on the bottom of the bag."

Julia rooted around and found the black rounded clips. But when the bleeding abated enough for them to see the edges of the wound, the hopes of using the Raney clips faded. She shook her head. "These won't work with a wound as jagged as this."

Still, now that she could see the injury clearly, the laceration was not as bad as she feared. She had expected such damage that the arm would be in danger of amputation. At the very least, she was expecting a Lifeflight helicopter ride to Moscow and microsurgery. But she had sewn up more serious muscle and skin traumas than this.

The wound began to bleed again, heavily. "Let's get him a 1% Lidocaine solution with epinephrine," she told Ben. "SubQ with a 27 needle. Those'll vasoconstrict the blood vessels and lessen the bleeding." She took over administering pressure to the brachial artery while Ben located the medication.

"Bunch of fuss over nothing," muttered Jake. Both she and Ben ignored the comment. Mabel hovered over, tears brimming her eyes.

Jake poised with the needle in hand. "Now Jake," he said. "This is going to hurt. We're injecting you with something that will help the bleeding, but it's the kind of stuff that's painful when it goes in. I'll go slowly so I don't make it too bad."

Jake nodded. But within moments of the needle slipping into his skin, he jerked and cursed. "What the hell are you doing? Son of a bitch, that hurts worse than the damn chain saw!"

Julia practically sat on him to keep him from thrashing. "Stupid bitch, get off me!" he yelled. She sat more firmly and jerked her head toward Mabel, indicating that she should calm her husband down.

Mabel knelt by Jake's head. "Hush, honey, they're just trying to help you," she murmured, and stroked his hair.

"Make 'em stop, Mabel," he moaned. But he grew still under his wife's hands, and Ben finished injecting the Lidocaine. "There. That's done, Jake, and you'll do better now."

Julia injected a local anesthetic, and she and Ben began cleaning the ugly gash. It took a lot to remove the debris left from the chain saw, but until the excess blood and dirt was removed, they were unable to gauge how serious the wound was.

"This is going to take a lot to fix up," said Ben at last. He stretched out his healing leg to ease the cramped position from attending to Jake while he was lying on the floor. "Frankly, Jake, this is beyond me. You're stabilized now, so we're going to take you back to the clinic in Jasper, then Medivac you to the hospital in Moscow from there."

"No!" Jake jerked his head up, and a thin trickle of blood spurted from the barely congealing arm. "You ain't getting me to one of those big-city hospitals! I ain't never been in one of those before, and I ain't starting now."

"But Jake, this is a deep wound, beyond my capabilities. If we don't get it properly stitched up by an expert, and check for nerve and tendon damage, you could lose use of the arm or even the arm itself."

Mabel gasped, but Jake ignored her. "Just do your best, doc, 'cuz I ain't going to no city hospital."

"Now Jake, you don't want to lose your arm over stubbornness, do you?"

"Just sew me up and I'll be fine."

Julia was faintly amazed that Ben considered this injury beyond his capabilities. "There's no need to Medivac him to Moscow," she told Ben. "See this? He cut much of the brachio-radialis, but not entirely. Both the median and the ulnar nerve are uncut. Suture a few of those veins, tie up the radialis and I think he'll be okay. If he refuses to go to the hospital, we'll have to patch him up here."

"You think you can handle it?"

"Yes."

"But you're a woman!" protested Jake.

Julia smiled as prettily as she could through clenched teeth. "That's right; Mr. Smothers, but I know what to do to get you stitched together. There won't be any reason for you to go to the hospital in Moscow if you don't want to."

But Jake stiffened and glared at her. "I ain't having no woman doctor pretend she knows what she's doing! You git away from me!"

Julia never recognized what an actress she was. Inside she was furious at his misogynistic attitude. Outside, she was the top graduate from the Julia Chambers School of Fake Charm.

"Come now, Mr. Smothers," she said with her most enchanting smile. "Haven't you ever heard about a woman's touch? Why, I'll fix you up so in a few months you never knew you had an accident with that chain saw."

She saw his eyes flicker with uncertainty to Ben and back to her. He glanced up at his wife, who murmured, "Let her, Jake. You need your arm."

So, grumbling and sour, he consented.

It took her three hours, working under such primitive conditions, to get Jake's arm sewn up. She seethed and stewed and thought black thoughts about the stubborn fool she was working on, but let none of her anger show.

With Ben following her terse directions, she irrigated the wound with saline and a disinfectant. She trimmed the skin to make an even edge. She carefully sutured the torn and cut muscles after debriding the tissue that wouldn't heal. She used absorbable sutures internally on the veins and muscle, and was finally able to close the wound.

Afterwards, Mabel Smothers wept with

gratitude. Patting the distraught woman on the back, Julia gave instructions for aftercare. Ben promised to bring a prescription of antibiotics the next day. Jake managed to give a muttered, "Thank you, ma'am," before she left.

It was pitch dark when the left the Smothers' house. Julia asked Ben to drive home.

Maneuvering down the rutted dirt road, he said, "That was fine doctoring, Julia. I congratulate you."

She didn't reply. She was too furious.

He glanced over. "What's the matter?" he asked in a puzzled voice.

"What a *jackass!*" she exploded.

"Who?"

"Jake Smothers, that's who! How *dare* he assume I'm incompetent because I'm a woman!"

"Oh, that."

She glared at him. "Yes, *that*. God, it was all I could to do smile at the bastard and fix his damn arm, when what I *really* wanted to do was break it."

"Julia, calm down."

"Calm *down?* When he nearly refused to let me operate on him because I have two X chromosomes and he has a Y? Aarrrgh!" She threw up her arms in a gesture of frustration.

"That's just Jake. He's an old-fashioned fellow with old-fashioned ideas."

"Well, his old-fashioned ideas could have cost him his arm."

"Yes, it could have. It was only the mercy of Providence that you were there, and managed to save it. So I'll say it again: that was fine doctoring. What you did was *way* beyond my skills. Where did you learn such techniques, anyway?"

"Hmmmph." She stared out at the dark conifers lit only by the headlights. It was endless and spooky out there in the forest. She was glad she wasn't driving this road alone. "I did my surgery rotation

65

under Stan Wyerson at Portland. He's a top-notch surgeon specializing in deep-wound traumas. I enjoyed that rotation. I liked patching people up, taking a limb that could have been amputated and bringing it back to life and usefulness."

She knew her tone was still grumpy, the sort a kid adopts when they're reluctantly acknowledging a compliment but want to stay grumpy.

Ben smiled. "Well, my hat's off to Stan Wyerson, whoever he is. He taught you well."

"Hmmmph," she said again. She crossed her arms and stared out at the dark forest.

"Hungry?"

She blew out a breath to release some tension. "Starved," she admitted. "I had lunch at a Chinese restaurant in Moscow this afternoon. It seems like days ago."

"The pizza place is closed. Nothing in this town stays open past nine o'clock. Let's go to my place—I can heat something up."

"Fine." A tiny little part of her was pleased, in fact. It was hard to admit that she wanted to get to know Ben better, and seeing him in his home environment was a good start.

"Look, an elk," said Ben suddenly. He slowed the car.

On the side of the road stood a giant deer with antlers encased in velvet. Julia had never seen such a creature before. "It's huge!" she gasped.

"Not nearly as huge as a bull moose, which is what I hit on my motorcycle."

He slowed the car and brought it to a stop. The forest around them was dark as ink, and the animal stood gleaming in the headlights of the car. He seemed unaffected by the headlights or the proximity of the car. He lowered his head to nibble at the leaves of a bush before crossing the road with stately strides and disappearing into the darkness.

"Wow," breathed Julia. "Now *that's* not something you see every day in Portland."

"They're something, aren't they?" Ben stepped on the accelerator, and they drove the rest of the way into Jasper.

The little town seemed deserted. Julia suspected she could cross the street without even looking for traffic. What she wouldn't give for a lively business strip, with a few good restaurants and maybe a nice coffee house or two. And some clothing stores. A bookstore, perhaps. Maybe some boutiques...

Ben's house was a pretty little cabin-style one-story structure on the edge of town, three blocks from the clinic. It was dark. When they emerged from the car, they heard Gypsy give a bark from the fenced backyard.

Ben limped up the steps more heavily than usual, Julia noted. She suspected his leg was hurting, especially after kneeling and sitting for three hours on a floor doing surgery.

"Go let Gypsy in, will you?" he asked, flipping on lights. "I'll get a fire going—it's chilly in here."

The enormous dog was glad to see someone. "No, down, Gypsy! Man, you're huge. Okay, here, I'll pet you." The canine wiggled in excitement and submitted to a few pats before dashing into the living room to greet her master.

Julia groped around and found the light for the kitchen. It was an old-fashioned room, with an ancient round-shouldered refrigerator and a sink that dripped.

"So." Ben limped into the kitchen. "I haven't had a chance to restock the kitchen since getting out of the chair, so I'm limited in what I can offer." He opened the fridge door and snapped open the small interior freezer. "What'll it be? I have microwave lasagna, microwave chicken, or microwave beef stew."

67

"Oh gosh, the anticipation..." Julia tapped her chin. "How about the lasagna?"

"Lasagna it is. And just to show what a terrific guy I am, I'll microwave yours first."

Julia wandered into the living room while he fiddled with the instant dinners. A single lamp lit the room along with the flames in the woodstove. The walls were lined with bookshelves, there were newspapers strewn untidily on the floor, and rural prints on the walls similar to what he had in his office at the clinic.

A pile of soiled socks sat in a corner as if he kicked them off every evening when he got home and seldom bothered to gather them up. A stereo with a shelf of CD's was wedged in among the books. Two overstuffed brown leather sofas looked inviting. It was a very masculine room—every inch a bachelor's place.

"Nice place," she said as Ben came out of the kitchen.

"I like it. Glass of wine?"

"Are we on call tonight?"

"We're always on call except when InstaDoc comes through."

"Then I'd better not. I'm a cheap date where wine is concerned."

His eyes gleamed. "I'll have to remember that. Here then—I've got some sparkling cider. I need to toast your medical expertise."

She followed him into the kitchen where he popped the top of a bottle of cider and poured some into wine glasses. He lifted his glass in salute. "To a fine piece of surgery if I ever saw it. Thanks for saving him, Julia."

"Thanks." She clicked glasses, touched by his tribute. His eyes were dark and intense, and she shivered with...something.

They tucked into their marginal food, both

hungry. Afterward, they went into the living room and sat on the sofas, watching the flames flicker in the woodstove. Gypsy snored at Ben's feet.

"Okay, let's talk about today," said Ben. "Why were you so angry on the drive home? This goes deeper than just a backwoodsman's attitude toward women, doesn't it?"

"Maybe." Julie avoided Ben's eyes and kept her gaze on the woodstove.

"Well?"

She glanced over at him. "Well what? Do you expect me to be dancing a jig because I was insulted, even while trying to save his life? Or at least his arm."

"No. But welcome to the world of difficult patients. They're everywhere."

"They seem especially thick around here," she muttered.

"Nah, they're no thicker here than anywhere else."

Julia snapped her glass onto the coffee table so hard that some of the sparkling cider splashed out. "Dammit, Ben, can't you see how *backwards* this place is?"

He raised his chin. "We're no more backwards than Portland. Or anywhere else."

She threw up her arms. "Sometimes this place reminds me of a third-world country!"

His brows snapped down. "Is that *your* opinion or...someone else's?"

"What do you mean?"

"I mean that you seem to be having a knee-jerk reaction to Jasper in general and the people who live here in particular. So I ask again: is it *you* who thinks Jasper is a third-world country...or someone else who convinced you of it?"

"That's *bullshit*, Ben."

"Look, doctors often have to deal with the
69

underbelly of a population anyway..."

"Ha. You got *that* right."

He glared at her. "Julia, you have *got* to get over this snobbery of yours. Just because not everyone has a college degree—"

"I'm not talking about education! But look around you—it seems that every other case involves wife beating or drug use or misogynists who refuse to go to the hospital even when their arm is nearly cut off! What is *with* this place, anyway?"

Ben's face darkened into a scowl. "I might ask what is with *you*, Julia?"

"Don't give me that. It's not my attitude that's the problem here. It's the attitude of the people. A woman who thinks I'm out to poison her kid just because I want to protect him from polio..."

"I *told* you there was some reluctance about vaccinations here..."

"Yeah, well, you didn't tell me that some bastard would rather lose his arm than let me operate on it."

"Well he let you, didn't he?"

"Sure. After I put on the Sweetness and Light display and fluttered my eyelashes. Though why that would convince him, I don't know."

Ben jerked to his feet and glowered down at her. Gypsy raised her head and blinked at them sleepily. "Are you so ready to write off the whole town, then, just because Jake Smothers was in pain and shock and said nasty things?" he nearly shouted. "Is that the sign of a competent doctor, Julia? Because if so, maybe you should head back to Portland—" He whirled around and gasped in pain. His face went white.

Julia was on her feet in an instant. "Sit down," she ordered, and helped him over to the sofa. "You've been pushing that leg too much today."

He grunted as he sat and stretched the healing leg out in front of him. He dropped his head against

Patrice Moore

the sofa back and closed his eyes, nostrils flaring.

Julia watched him, hating to see someone hurting. "What pain medication are you on? Naprosin?"

"Yes."

"Where is it?"

"In the bedroom, on the bedside table."

"Hang on. I'll get it."

She darted toward the archway of what must lead to the bedrooms. She flipped on the bedroom light and got an impression of yet another masculine enclave, with an unmade bed and piles of clothes on the floor, more stacks and shelves of books and a dresser with one drawer half-open.

The sight of the bed—tousled, somehow intimate—made her avert her eyes as she snatched up the bottle of Naprosin and hurried back to the living room. Ben still had his eyes closed. It seemed he was concentrating on mastering the pain and not admitting just how much the leg must hurt.

She glanced at the label and tipped out two tablets. "Here," she said quietly. She handed him the tablets and his glass of cider. "This will help."

"Thanks." He swallowed the tablets and leaned forward to put the glass on the coffee table. "I guess sitting on the floor for three hours while helping you with surgery wasn't the best thing I could have done for the leg."

"No kidding." She perched on the edge of the sofa and sighed. "Ben, I'm sorry. I should warn you that I sometimes have a hot temper. Jake Smothers just rubbed me the wrong way, I guess."

"Despite his eccentricities, he's not a bad guy," said Ben. He gave her a wan smile. "And though *you* couldn't tell, *I* could see that he was impressed with you. Deeply so." He moved his leg a fraction and winced.

"Stop moving it," she ordered. Without thinking,

71

she rested her hands on his leg to keep it still. "Have you done your physical therapy exercises on it today?"

"No. Got too busy."

She shook her head. "Doctors make the worst patients," she muttered. "You need to take better care of it during your recuperation. Will it help to massage it?"

"Yes, actually. My orthopedic surgeon recommended it, in fact."

"Let me, then."

If someone had asked her, Julia would have argued that her actions were purely medicinal, motivated by nothing more than a desire to heal. Of course that was it.

But despite the firmness of her hands on his healing muscles, Julia was pleased at the excuse to touch him. She kept her face averted as she worked up and down his leg, massaging the muscles with strong and powerful and controlled actions.

"That feels good," murmured Ben as she pressed and kneaded the muscles, alternating between the gastrocnemius and quadriceps.

"That's the idea."

"You're good at this."

"Like I said, I enjoyed my physical therapy rotation. I seem to have a knack for it."

"No argument here."

There was silence for a few moments while the fire snapped in the woodstove, casting flickering light on the wall. Gypsy gave a sleepy sigh and shifted her position on the carpet. And still Julia continued to massage the leg.

"Look, I understand how you feel about being here," said Ben at last. "I felt the same way too, when I took over the clinic."

She stared at him. "How could you feel the same way? You were eager to repay the town for putting you through med school, remember?"

"Of course I remember. But what I haven't mentioned is that I was resentful as hell for the obligation I had to pay back."

"What do you mean? I thought you liked it here."

"I do. Now. But not at first. After all, I left this place as a kid. A teenager. I was a typical adolescent in that I felt there was nothing to do in this backwater place. I wanted action, excitement, adventure, and Los Angeles—which is where I went to med school—provided that. But there was this stupid obligation, dammit."

She moved her hands back up to his quad and kneaded the muscle. "So what happened?"

He gave a small snort. "What happened was that I found I had grown up. I left Jasper as a rebellious teen. I came back as a mature man, and I could look at what I had taken for granted when I was younger and appreciate it more."

"And what was it you had taken for granted?" Julia asked in sincere wonder.

"Oh Julia...you haven't even seen half what this place has to offer. Sure, some of the people are—well, difficult. Different. But there's a warmth and genuineness to so many people out here that you won't find in a big city. Folks haven't been altered by some of civilization's more unpleasant developments. Yes, we have a meth problem, and no, Jasper isn't perfect, but it's not bad."

"So it's the people who make it for you?"

"Partly. I work with people, of course, so that's part of it. And there's something to be said for being a big fish in a small pond. I'm one of the best-liked and best-respected men in the town. I've brought babies into this world, children of my schoolmates, and I like the idea of watching those babies grow into young men and women. Some will go through teen rebellion and leave Jasper. Some will stay away, some will come home again. There's a continuity here that's hard to find elsewhere."

"How long did it take you to adjust?"

"About a year."

"Oh." Her hands grew still for a moment, then resumed. "A lot longer than I'll be here."

Things fell silent for awhile as she continued her ministrations. Her thoughts drifted from the difficulties in her present job, then to Ben's words about adjusting, then to Ben himself.

Her hands were getting a little tired from the strong kneading she gave his muscles, but she didn't want to give up.

"Julia," said Ben softly.

Startled at his change in tone, she looked up. In the half-light cast by the single lamp and the fire, he looked dark and attractive and...well, desirable.

"What?" she whispered.

"You're enjoying this, aren't you?"

Her hands slowed and then stopped, though she didn't remove them from his leg. "You mean the massaging?"

"Yes."

"Well...why do you ask?"

"Because maybe it's just me, but I detect a certain, well, enthusiasm about this."

"But doesn't it feel good?"

"It feels outstanding," he said quietly. "And not just from a medicinal standpoint."

She yanked her hands away. "What do you mean?" Unwittingly her eyes dropped to a portion of his body that left no doubt to his meaning. She jerked her eyes up to his.

He leaned forward, reducing the distance between them to mere inches. His eyes were dark, intense, and heavy-lidded with desire. She didn't pull back.

"Kiss me, Julia," he whispered.

74

She hesitated for the space of a heartbeat. She knew that her decision in the next moment would alter their working relationship forever. Did she want that? Did she dare plunge into the unknown after Alex's betrayal? Did she—

Shut up, Julia, she thought.

She closed the distance between them and met his lips. Her eyes fluttered closed as a soaring sensation blossomed inside her. Passion flared with unexpected strength, and she made a small noise in the back of her throat.

It was awkward, kissing Ben while half-kneeling on the floor as she'd been doing, until he raised her up and nestled her in the crook of his arm. It was a tender gesture, at odds with the passion pouring from his lips against hers, and Julia melted into him. Silence reigned while they explored each other.

"Have you any idea how long I've wanted to do this?" he murmured at last, raining kisses across her face, neck, shoulders.

"No. How long?"

"From the first moment I laid eyes on you." He laid a butterfly kiss on the tip of her nose. "I wanted to tug those damn pins from your hair and let it down." His hands roamed up and touched the large knot of hair but didn't loosen it. "You're every man's walking fantasy, Julia."

His words chilled her despite the heat coursing through her body. She knew Ben could feel her withdrawal, for he pulled back. "What's wrong?"

She shook her head. "Just wary. You're an attractive man, Ben. But the last thing I want to do is complicate my life by having an affair with my boss."

"How would it complicate your life?"

She pulled entirely out of his arms. "You know so little about me, Ben. You don't know what my life was like before I came here. All you see is the package, the surface of me. In other words, you're talking about the physical attraction, nothing more."

"Well, it's a start." He smiled, but there was sadness behind the smile. "Does the leg put you off?"

"The leg?" For a moment Julia was genuinely puzzled. "You mean because you're recovering from an injury?" She stared at him, aghast. "Is that the kind of person you think I am?"

"Not necessarily. But there is a certain blow to the male ego when he knows he can't even make love to a woman without extreme pain."

"No, it's not your leg. At all. You should know me better than that..."

"You just told me I don't know you at all."

She took a deep breath. "It's not your injury. It's just that I'm not ready to plunge into an affair with you."

"It wasn't *just* an affair I was interested in."

"Even worse. I...I can't, Ben."

His eyes narrowed. "He must have really hurt you."

She gave a small jerk. "Who?"

"Whoever you left behind in Portland, that's who."

The chill deepened. "There's no one."

"That's a load of bull. It couldn't be plainer than if you shouted it from the rooftops. Someone hurt you bad enough that you're burned."

"That's none of your business." She stood up and nearly tripped over Gypsy, who was curled up near the sofa. "I'm going home. It's late. With luck we won't have any calls tomorrow and can have the whole day clear. Good night, Ben."

"You can't run away forever, Julia," called Ben. His words echoed into the night and mocked her as she ran for her car.

Chapter Five

Oh yes she *could* run away forever.

She'd run all through college. All through medical school. All through her internship. And then she'd stopped running and slammed into a brick wall during the first part of her residency when she met Alex. The resulting pain still reverberated through her.

Julia stomped into her house in a fine temper. The cat came trotting out of the bedroom and tried to curl around her legs, but Julia didn't slow down to pet him as she usually did. She paced up and down the small living room, her lips burning with the remembered kisses, her body tuned tight as a bowstring, wanting to make love to Ben.

But he would leave her. People always did. Her father did. Her mother did. Alex did. And Ben would too, if she let him get close to her.

That's why she hadn't named the cat. Even *he* would leave her if she let him get too close.

Abruptly she sat down on the sofa and dropped her head in her hands. How long? How long would she run? A lifetime of loneliness—a road of self-imposed isolation—stretched before her, empty and desolate and bleak. But at least it was a safe road.

I am a rock...I am an island...and a rock feels no pain. And an island never cries...

The words of the old Simon and Garfunkel song swam through her mind. She groaned and leaned back against the sofa. *A rock feels no pain.*

The cat jumped up and rubbed against her, his

77

purr running like a motor. Remorseful of her earlier brush-off, she scratched his neck.

"Maybe you're the ghost of Christmas past," she murmured. "Here to remind me what I've lost and what I've given up."

She leaned back and closed her eyes. Images from her past danced before her...unhappy images. Her father leaving when she was eight. Her mother abandoning her when she was sixteen, leaving her to finish high school billeted with friends. Her single-minded pursuit of higher education as a means of avoiding intimacy. And then came Alex.

Alex, with his flattering attention and gorgeous good looks and brilliant mind. Alex, picking away at her self-esteem as he highlighted her ignorance in everything from medicine to opera. Alex, telling her that she'd never make a good doctor if she couldn't handle the emotional aftermath of losing a patient. Alex, his handsome face contorted with disgust, walking out the door. Abandoning her. Deserting her. Leaving her.

A rock feels no pain...

A tear leaked out of the corner of her eye as she continued to pet the cat. *And an island never cries.*

****

Ben called the next morning, Sunday morning, pulling Julia out of the bathroom where she had just stepped from the shower. Naked, with a towel around her, she gave a sensuous shiver at hearing his voice.

"I'm going to run the antibiotics and some painkillers up to Jake Smothers," he said. "Do you want to go?"

"No."

"Are you avoiding Jake, or are you avoiding me?"

"Both."

"I see." There was a pause. "I'll pick you up in

half an hour."

"Ben...!" But the phone clicked dead.

Julia glared at the phone before hanging it up. Then she smiled. What a guy.

She had enough time to first walk to Betty's Café and get a large cup of coffee to go. Betty's coffee, she was learning, was even better than her soup.

She sat on her front step, sipping coffee, until Ben pulled up to her house. Her still-damp hair was pinned up. "Feeling a little high-handed this morning, aren't you?" she inquired as she climbed into the passenger seat.

"No. I just want you to understand that...well, what passed between us last night can't affect our professional obligations."

"I wasn't planning on letting it."

"But you were going to avoid coming today."

"Well..."

He threw her a glance. "I'm not about to apologize for what happened. I'm extremely attracted to you, Julia. I won't deny it. But nor will I push in where I'm not wanted." He gave a grimace. "Besides—physically, I can't."

Glad to have a distraction from the intimacy of where the conversation was going, Julia asked, "How's the leg?"

"Better, since you massaged it so well."

"Have you done your physical therapy exercises?"

"No. Not yet. I...well, I need help with them."

She threw him a glance. "You don't have to sound so happy about it!"

"Why not? It's a great excuse to have your hands on me again." He grinned. "After all, you *did* offer."

They headed out of town. Once they were on the rural highway heading toward the Smothers' farm, Jake suddenly pulled the car over to the side of the road.

"What the matter?" asked Julia, startled.

"Nothing." He turned in his seat, captured her face with his hands, and laid a sensual kiss on her lips that left her dizzy and breathless. In moments it was over, and he put the car in gear and started driving again as if nothing had happened.

Julia stared straight ahead, not sure what hit her, but knowing that her lips were throbbing and her heart was beating fast.

"Wh-what was that for?" she finally asked.

"Just thought I'd keep you off balance," he replied. His right wrist lay over the steering wheel, his left hand on the spokes in a casual pose.

She blew out a breath but said nothing. He had certainly accomplished his goal.

They didn't speak much on the twenty minute trip to the Smothers'. As they bumped over the rocky dirt road toward the house, Julia asked, "Does Jake Smothers know I'm along for the ride?"

"Don't know, don't care. You're working here now, Julia. You can't let some stubborn old fool intimidate you."

Ben was right, of course. Julia lifted her chin and prepared to do battle.

But there was no need. The moment she stepped foot inside the door, she was treated like a hero.

"There you are!" exclaimed Mabel Smothers. She gave Julia a shy hug and fresh tears sparkled in her weary blue eyes. "I don't know if I properly thanked you for what you did for Jake last night. He's doing much better. Come see him."

Julia and Ben followed Mabel down a short hall toward a bedroom. Jake lay in bed, propped up on pillows, watching television. He clicked off the screen the moment everyone walked in.

"Morning," he said gruffly.

Ben hung back, and Julia took her cue. "Good

morning, Mr. Smothers," she said, advancing into the room. "How are you feeling?"

"Better than I deserve." He straightened up further. "And embarrassed about my behavior last night. I owe you an apology, Dr. Chambers. Mabel's spent the last twelve hours calling me a dang fool for insulting the person who patched me together. Fact is, Doc, I could'a lost my arm because of my dad-blamed stubbornness. Mabel is right about that."

Julia felt the hard knob of resentment melt inside her. She knew just how much it cost the crusty man to make an admission like that.

"No hard feelings, then," she said. "Let's take a look and see how your arm is doing."

She unwrapped the bandages, checked for infection or fresh bleeding, applied some antibiotic ointment, and re-dressed the wound. "It's doing fine," she said. "We've brought you some painkillers. Don't hesitate to take some medicine if you're hurting—don't try to be tough or macho about it. And take these antibiotics to prevent infection." She handed him the bottle that Ben had brought. "Take all the pills according to the directions. *All* of them, do you hear? Even when you feel better and think you don't need them anymore." She smiled at him.

"I will." Jake Smothers glanced at his hovering wife. "Mabel will keep me on the straight and narrow."

"Good." Julia rose. "We'll check in with you every so often and make sure you're healing up as you should." She shook his hand and followed Mabel and Ben outside.

"I hope you don't mind, Dr. Chambers," said Mabel. "I made these for you. I—I hope you like 'em."

She handed Julia a brown paper bag. Inside were several dozen cookies of several different types.

"Wow! These look wonderful! Thank you."

Mabel bit her lip for a moment. "I don't think I

need to tell you how different our lives would be if Jake had lost the use of his arm. I near bit his head off for hollering at you yesterday."

"He was in pain and in shock," soothed Julia. "He probably doesn't even remember much of what he said."

"That's a fact, but it don't excuse his behavior. We'll be passin' 'round the word what a good doctor you are, miss. Thanks for coming back to check on us."

Julia leaned back in the car seat as Ben drove away. "Well. That was a change of attitude."

"Told you." Ben gave a smirk.

She punched him playfully on the arm. "Know-it-all."

"I don't know it *all*, but I know Jake. And Mabel. The man dotes on her, for all his gruff manner."

"I can tell." She sighed. "Quite a difference between Mabel Smothers and Mary Lansing."

The silence that fell on them was more at ease as they drove back toward Jasper. When they reached the place where they had seen the elk the night before, Ben slowed the car and pulled it off to the side of the road.

"What's the matter?" asked Julia, instantly wary. "You're not planning on throwing me off balance again, are you?"

"Nope. Thought I'd show you something interesting instead."

He grabbed his cane and got out of the car as Julia did the same. The walked off the road into the dark forest.

It was a beautiful, cloudless day, but the blue sky arching overhead could barely be seen because of the denseness of the conifers. Shafts of sunlight pierced the canopy and highlighted the needled ground. They walked for perhaps five minutes before the land started to slope sharply. Then they came to

82

a break in the trees, and Julia saw the lake.

"Wow," she breathed.

The view showed the distant blue waters of Lake Percheron. Before them, the terrain angled into a large gorge, heavily treed and beautiful. It was a postcard snapshot, a real Kodak moment.

"Look up there," Ben said, and pointed. "A bald eagle."

"Really!" She stared, awed, at the majestic bird perched on the bare branches of a dead tree. "I've never seen one outside of a zoo."

"They're all over the place up here. I've seen as many as seven on one tree down by the lake."

"This would be *some* view by the light of a full moon," she murmured, gazing at the distant lake. She knew Ben was watching her expression.

"Maybe I'll show you that some time. Just a taste of what this place is like," he added. "People actually come here on vacation because it's so beautiful. And *I'm* lucky enough to live here."

Without another word he turned and started limping back toward the car. Julia feasted on the view for another moment, then turned and followed.

"Now I'm going to show you my favorite beach," he said, as he started the car and continued down the rural highway. Julia noted that they hadn't passed another car since leaving the Smothers'.

"Shouldn't we be getting back?"

"Why? Got anything pressing to do today?"

"Well, no—"

"Then let me show you around. We've both got our cell phones—if someone needs us, they'll call."

He drove until they were about two miles outside of Jasper, then took a narrow paved road to the right. A sign announced "Jasper Point" ahead, along with schematics showing swimming, picnicking, and camping facilities.

"I doubt there'll be anyone here," he said. "It's

still early in the season and too cold to swim, and that's what usually brings people out here."

They parked the car and walked down a dirt trail. Ben moved slowly because of his leg. The trees parted at the bottom of the trail to reveal a cove of gravel sloping gently into the lake waters. Trees ringed the deserted beach. The lake stretched before them, large and blue and sparkling. A plain wooden dock extended a hundred feet over the water.

"Pretty," said Julia. It was a massive understatement.

"I love this place. It's not as popular a beach as Rocky Point is, across the water over there." He pointed, and Julia could make out another cove, with boat slips and boat houses surrounding it. "But it's quieter here, and more peaceful. Often in the summer I'll just bring my fishing pole and a good book, and spend hours here." He flashed a grin. "Until I'm pulled away by my beeper, of course."

"How deep is the water here?" Julia started walking out on the dock. Ben followed, leaning heavily on his cane and watching his footing on the uneven boards. She walked to the end of the dock and looked into the green water.

"Not sure. I'm guessing ten feet or so. Look— over there." He stepped up behind her.

"What are they?"

"Swans. Tundra swans."

"Five, six, seven, eight of them," she counted. "I don't believe it. My first wild elk, my first bald eagle, my first swans—all in the space of twenty-four hours."

"I counted seventeen here once time," he said. From behind, he snaked his arms around her waist and rested his chin on her shoulder as he gazed over the water. "They seem to like to gather in late spring like this."

"Wh-what are you doing?" she whispered.

"Enjoying the view."

She bit her lip. It felt right—so incredibly right—to stand looking over the solitary water at a flock of swans on a fresh spring day with a handsome man holding her around the waist. There was nothing sexual in his embrace...except in her mind.

How long they stood there, suspended in time, she couldn't guess. Then they were interrupted by the bane of every doctor...the cell phone.

Ben groaned. "Damn. And I was so comfortable, too. —Is that yours or mine?"

"Mine." Flustered, Julia dug into her pocket and pulled out her cell phone. She flipped it up and said, "Hello?"

"Hi Julia, it's Alex."

Her eyes widened in dismay. Her ex-fiancé...why was he calling her?

She stepped away from Ben and turned her back for a modicum of privacy. She kept her voice neutral. "Well, hi. This is a surprise. How are you?"

"Fine. Busy. On call, as usual. Listen, Julia—I talked to Pat Schwietzer at the hospital. He's willing to put you on as a Resident with me to do your last rotation in internal medicine. Isn't that terrific?"

"With *you?*" she gasped.

"Yes, with *me*," he bit back, with a touch of sarcasm. "After all, you haven't done internal medicine yet, and you may as well go with the best. I volunteered to take you on and Schwietzer agreed."

"Hooray for him." Julia couldn't keep the bitterness from her voice.

"You don't sound overly excited about this."

Julia moved down the dock away from Ben. "Alex, you walked out on me when I needed you most. Now tell me why I should be happy to be doing a rotation with you?"

"Because *you're* the one who wanted to be a GP,"

85

he snapped. "If you're going to go that route, you may as well have the best training you can have."

"Meaning with you."

"Of course. Unless you want to go to San Francisco—there are a number of good internists there."

"Why can't I stay here to finish my training?" Julia stepped off the end of the dock and walked along the gravel beach. A quick glance at Ben showed that he was facing the water, politely giving her the illusion of privacy. However, she knew he was probably straining to hear everything. Heck, *she* would have, in his place.

Axes gave a guffaw at the thought. "C'mon, Julia. As if you can get anything but basic training in place like Jasper, Idaho."

"My training is going just fine, thank you. I'm spending my days doing everything from helping kids with anaphylactic shock to patching up chain saw accidents. I'm not sure about you, but that strikes me as excellent GP training."

Alex gave another laugh—Julia suddenly remembered how annoying those elitist laughs could be—and said, "I can't believe you're actually thinking about staying in a place like Jasper beyond your three-month rotation. You need to complete your training with more concentrated situations."

"Alex, it *is* concentrated here. Why are patients any different in Portland than they are in Jasper?"

"I don't believe this. Are you *defending* that little backwater?" There was a note of incredulity in his voice.

"Maybe I am." Maybe she was. What a difference two weeks could make.

"Julia, I want you to think seriously about this. Your career could be on the line here."

"What difference does it make to *you?*" she snapped. "My career is of no concern to you. You forfeited that when you broke off with me."

"Julia," said Alex, and there was a quieter tone to his voice. "That's another reason why I called. I might have been too hasty about breaking up with you."

"I don't believe this!" she groaned. "Don't tell me you're going to start talking about reinstating our engagement!"

"Look, I realize I hurt you after—after you lost that patient. But I'm asking you to consider letting bygones be bygones."

"So you can have me back in your bed, is that it?"

"Well, you must admit we were good together."

"Right, until things got tough for me and you dropped me like a hot potato."

"We can talk about that later. For now, though, I think you'll agree that I'm the best option for you to complete your residency."

"Alex, I'm going to hang up now," said Julia. Her insides were churning, and it was all she could do to keep her voice level. "I'll think about what you said, but I'm not going to make any decisions now. Goodbye."

She hung up before he could protest. She shoved her cell phone in her pocket and stared unseeing across the water, fists clenched. It took a few moments to realize that her insides were churning not from torment or regret, but from anger.

She heard a noise behind her and whipped around to see Ben limping her way. She'd forgotten about him—hadn't even seen him walking down the dock back toward the beach.

"Everything okay?" he asked quietly.

"Fine." She spat the word out.

He quirked an eyebrow. "I'll beg to differ, but I know better than to ask questions at the moment." He turned toward the trail. "Ready to head home?"

She looked at his back as he made his way toward the trail to the parking lot, rooted in surprise. Perversely she wanted him to inquire about the phone call so she could scream and holler and take out her anger on him. And dammit, all he did was "know better than to ask questions at the moment." Aarrrgghh!!

She stomped back to the car with little grace and was silent on the ride home. Ben dropped her off with a simple, "See you tomorrow," and left her to stew on her own.

And stew she did. She recalled all the times she'd had with Alex—his flattering attention during her rotations, his help in mastering some difficult studies, his lovemaking. His head-turning good looks. His condescension. His sardonic laughter.

And—inevitably—she compared him to Ben. Ben's laughter was never sardonic. His looks were handsome but not stunning. He seemed understanding and sympathetic.

But what, really, did she know of Ben? She'd met him only two weeks ago. She'd heard Sandra's story about his background, but that was it. There was no bad hearsay or scandals that she was aware of. He seemed to be just as he appeared: a deeply caring, well-liked member of the community.

Next to Alex, he was a piece of honest, everyday quartz next to a glittering piece of gold.

Was that such a bad thing?

****

Her mood was precarious at best the next day, Monday. She went through her appointments with a clench-teethed hold on her temper and her emotions. But she got through the day without losing it.

That evening she stopped at the grocery store before going home. In front of the vegetable section, she saw Mary Lansing.

"Mrs. Lansing!" she exclaimed, touching the

other woman on the shoulder. Mary Lansing jumped when Julia touched her shoulder, then smiled and relaxed when she saw Julia. "Dr...Chambers, right?"

"Yes." Mary's eye had healed except for a faint bruising underneath, and she didn't flinch as Julia shook her hand. "I'm glad to see you. How are you feeling?"

"Fine. I'm fine." She ducked her head and looked at the floor.

"Are you really fine, Mrs. Lansing?" asked Julia gently. "Has your husband been hurting you any more?"

"No. Really, he hasn't." Mary Lansing turned and reached for an onion, and in doing so used her left hand which had two fingers bound together in a homemade splint. Caught in her lie, she snatched her hand against her body and turned her back.

"Look, Mary." Julia turned her around and took her by the shoulders. "I want you to get into a battered women's shelter in Moscow. I looked into them, and there are two available. I can drive you in anytime. Tonight, if you wish."

"No."

"Why not?"

"I—I can't leave Lenny."

"But why? Why stay with a man who is hurting you?"

"He doesn't hurt me all the time. Most of the time he's fine."

"Except when he's not." The bubbling anger that Julia had been feeling since Alex's call started to overflow. She dropped her hands from Mary's shoulders and jammed them into her pockets in a gesture of frustration. "I don't understand why you can't walk out of a situation like that."

"Because I love him."

Out of the corner of her eye, Julia saw someone turn the corner into the vegetable section, and she tried to keep her voice low. "But I'm not so sure how much he loves you back if he's breaking your fingers and giving you black eyes. Mrs. Lansing, I'm sure you know that men like that only get worse..."

"No. Please. I can't." Mary Lansing threw up her hands as if to ward Julia off, and started backing away. She bumped into a vegetable bin, turned, and fled.

Julia blew out a breath, and closed her eyes while she pinched the bridge of her nose. She had done it again—sent Mary Lansing fleeing.

"You've got to stop pressuring her, Julia," said a voice.

Her eyes snapped open to see Ben. "What are *you* doing here?"

"Grocery shopping, of course. Julia, leave Mary alone. She'll go to a shelter when she's ready."

Julia clenched her fists. "How can she *stay* with the bastard? He broke her fingers this time. And she says she *loves* him!"

"She'll leave when she can't take it any more."

"Sure. When she has a broken arm or something." She turned and picked up an onion and slammed it into her cart.

"Knock it off, Julia," said Ben in a stern voice. "You have to learn how to handle these people."

"Dammit, how can you be so *passive* about this!" she cried, furious.

Ben glanced around him, then took her by the arm. "The grocery store is not the place to talk about this," he gritted. "Let's get out of here."

Five minutes later they entered Ben's house. Gypsy danced around, happy to have a visitor.

"Now what's this all about?" asked Ben. "It's not just Mary. You've been tense as a bowstring all day."

"Look, I'm just pissed that she's getting the crap beat out of her, and you won't be proactive about helping her!"

"Mary Lansing is all grown up, in case you haven't noticed," he said. "Just what do you think I can do—proactively—to help her, against her wishes?"

Julia opened her mouth, then shut it with a snap. She huffed out a breath and ran a hand through her hair. "Hell, I don't know."

"Neither do I. You know, Julia, your problem is that you care too much. It makes you lose patience. *And* patients," he added with a small smile, apparently pleased with his pun.

"I don't want to deal with a future homicide case," muttered Julia.

"We won't be. The local police are looking to break up a meth ring in the area. Lenny is probably involved, just as you suggested. I'm cooperating with the police as much as I can. But for now, Mary Lansing is choosing to live with this situation, so until she wants to get out, we can't help her. Besides," he added. He crossed his arms and looked at her. "Mary's just the scapegoat here. What's *really* bothering you?"

"Nothing."

"Don't give me that. You've been bent out of shape ever since that phone call yesterday afternoon. Who was it?"

"It was personal. None of your business."

"Of course it's my business."

Julia glared at him. "On what grounds can you *possibly* claim it's your business?"

"On the grounds that it's affecting your professional performance. Cornering a battered woman in the grocery store and trying to bully her into going to a shelter is starting to cross the line."

"I don't believe this!" She threw up her arms. "You think I was *wrong* to try to talk Mary into a shelter?"

"I think it was ill-timed and in an inappropriate

place. Besides, you're getting off the subject. Why were you so upset after that phone call?"

She crossed her arms. "I'm not planning on telling you, so you can just stop interrogating me about it."

"Julia." He crossed over to her and took her by the shoulders. His voice was gentle. "I told you before—I'm very attracted to you. As such, I have an interest in anything that is upsetting you. Can't you tell me what it is?"

She bit her lip and dropped her gaze as tears sprang to her eyes. How long had it been since she's seen tenderness in a man?

Clem Parker had shown this emotion when he gathered his daughter into his arms, and it had brought tears to her eyes. And here was Ben, offering her the same kind of compassion. Trouble was, she didn't know how to handle it.

Ben led her over to the couch. He sat down and drew her stiff body into a loose embrace against his shoulder. He said nothing, and she knew he was merely letting her come to terms with whatever was troubling her.

She sighed. "Ben, maybe you have a better technique than I do. Whenever I'm bothered by something, I want to take the bull by the horns and wrestle it out of them, like with Mary Lansing. But you—you weasel it out by gentle persuasion."

"Hey, whatever works."

"Okay, you win." She pulled out of Ben's arm and settled back against the couch so she didn't have to look him in the eye. "The person on the phone yesterday was a fellow named Alex Rudolph. He— he's my ex-fiancé."

She felt Ben stiffen beside her. "I see."

"Let me emphasize that again: *ex*-fiancé. He's an internist at Portland City Hospital where I did most of my residency. He called to tell me that he had made arrangements to do my internal medicine rotation with him."

"And you said...?"

"I said I'd think about it. What I *really* wanted to do was to tell him to go to hell."

He chuckled. "Well put."

"Not that it may do much good. I might be called back to Portland to work under him regardless. But that's not all. He...well, he wanted to open up the idea of us getting back together. No doubt that's why he arranged for me to do my rotation with *him*, as opposed to any other internist. Except, of course, that he's the best internist between San Francisco and the Canadian border, in his opinion."

"Oh—one of those. A specialist who thinks he's God."

"That's it. He made the expected derogatory remarks that whatever kind of measly training I'm getting in this little backwater burg can't possibly match what he's arranging for me. As if my career is of any concern to him. He thinks GP work is a cop-out."

"You can't become a GP if you're not a people-person," commented Ben.

Amazed at this insightful remark, Julia glanced over at him. "Well, that sums it up nicely! Alex most definitely isn't a 'people-person.' He thinks most people are below him, so he'd be a terrible GP. At some level I think he recognizes that, and so he derides the field."

"No offense and all, Julia, but what did you *see* in the guy?"

She sighed again. "In retrospect, good question. He's gorgeous, of course, and has self-confidence oozing out his pores. I was flattered at his attention. He was the first serious relationship I'd ever had."

"And he spoiled you for other men."

She didn't look at him. "For the moment, yes.

I'm still healing from the sting."

There was silence for a few moments. Then Julia added, "But Ben, you may as well know…I may not have much choice about returning to Portland and doing my internist rotation there."

"I know, I know." Ben reached out and took her hand, which he held in his. "One of the banes of training to be a doctor. I was lucky that I did most of my training here, once I got done with all the specialty fields."

Comforted, Julia threaded her fingers through his. "I'll admit you're right. It helps to share what's upsetting me."

Ben chuckled. "See? You learn something new as a doctor every day."

"So…have you done your PT yet?"

"Ah, no. As I said, I needed your help. It's either that, or I have to go to Moscow to do it."

"No, that won't be necessary…*if* you promise to keep things strictly professional between us while I'm yanking your leg in all directions."

Ben rose to his feet and smiled down at her. "Believe me, the kind of shape I'll be in after you're done practically *insures* that I keep my hands and thoughts to myself. I'll barely be able to walk across the room when you're done."

Julia smiled. "Let's get started, then."

Chapter Six

Julia worked on Ben's physical therapy with diligence all week. The therapy was painful and left him with no desire to pursue any more intimate issues. But she could see how quickly he was improving. He even tried getting around without his cane.

"Dan's coming in tonight," said Ben on Thursday afternoon.

"Dan who?" asked Julia.

"Sorry. Dan Kendall, the circuit doctor I told you about. Y'know, InstaDoc. He comes in on Thursday nights every other weekend and stays until Tuesday morning." He gave a great sigh of relief. "Weekend off!"

"Just in time, too." Julia finished making a notation in a patient's file and slid it shut. "Sandra Kempke invited me to dinner tonight. Maybe I can relax and have a glass of wine if they offer, without worrying about being on call."

She told Ben about bumping into Sandra in Moscow, and the Chinese lunch they had shared. Naturally she didn't mention the topic of discussion that had occupied much of their meal.

"Me, I plan on going fishing with Gypsy this weekend," said Ben. "Care to join me?"

"Nope. I might go to Moscow or even to Lewiston or Spokane. Explore the region a bit more.

Julia left the clinic before Dan Kendall got there, though she intended to stop in over the weekend and introduce herself. She showered and dressed in slacks and a blouse for dinner at Sandra's. The weather was getting warmer now, and it was pleasant to wear lighter clothes.

Sandra and her husband Todd lived about a mile outside of town. They had a pretty, older house on an acre of land. Todd's sheriff's car was parked in the driveway—the practice, Julia now knew, of rural sheriff's officers. Two blossoming trees adorned the front yard, and an old detached garage had been converted to a woodshop. Julia knew this because as she drove up, she heard the noise of power equipment and a mist of fine sawdust wafted from the building.

"Hi," said Sandra, giving Julia a little hug over her expanding girth. "Thanks for coming to dinner. You look great."

Julia would have liked to say the same thing, but she choked on her reply. Sandra looked pale and wan. Her face had swollen since her last appointment, and she kept putting her hand to her forehead.

"Sandra, you look sick as a dog," said Julia, alarmed. She took the pregnant woman by the arm and led her to a chair. "What's been going on lately?"

"Well, I've been vomiting," admitted Sandra. "I thought I was all done with that, and then it started up again."

"Are you feeling pain or tenderness here?" Julia touched Sandra's upper abdomen.

"Yeah. Sort of."

"Oh Sandra," groaned Julia. "You should have come into the clinic."

"No. I'm fine, really I am...oh Julia, this is my husband Todd. Todd, Dr. Julia Chambers."

Todd Kempke stood on the front porch and brushed off the excess sawdust before reaching over to shake hands. He had the strapping build of a sheriff who stays in shape. "Pleased to meet you, Dr.

Chambers..."

"Julia, please."

"Julia, then. Sandra's been talking up a storm about you." He dropped a kiss on his wife's head and they all moved into the living room.

"I've been looking forward to coming tonight," said Julia.

"Me too," said Sandra. "I've been telling Todd about how nice it is to have a woman doctor in town."

"Though if it's all the same to you, I'll keep getting my physicals done with Ben," said Todd, and winked at Julia.

A timer chimed in the kitchen. "That'll be the potatoes done," said Sandra. "I'm going to check on dinner—be right back." She waddled from the room, and Julia followed her with her eyes.

"A glass of wine, Julia?" asked Todd.

"I'd love one, thanks," said Julia, "but I won't."

Todd's hand suspended above the wine bottle. "Why not? Sandra said you weren't on call tonight."

"That's right." Julia glanced toward the kitchen door. "But Todd, I'll be honest—Sandra looks pretty bad. I'm worried about her."

Todd turned pale and set the wine bottle down. "Worried in what way?"

"Worried about her pre-eclampsia. As you know, it can be a dangerous condition. She admitted to having some symptoms that concern me."

"Like what?"

"Like vomiting. And some pain in her midsection. I'd feel more comfortable if you'd check her into Gritman in Moscow."

"But Ben said she should go in around her thirty-seventh week. She's only at thirty-four right now."

There was a crash and a small scream from the kitchen. Frozen for an instant, Julia met Todd's eyes and saw fear. Then they both dashed toward the kitchen.

Sandra stood gripping the counter, ash-pale, with a shattered dish in the sink and a pool of liquid at her feet. "My water broke!" she gasped.

"It's just as I feared," muttered Julia. "Todd, take her and lay her down on the couch. I'm calling Ben." Her hands were shaking as she dug her cell phone out of her pocket.

"Oh God, stop those lights," moaned Sandra. "They're too bright."

"C'mon, Ben, *answer*," gritted Julia, as the line rang. She stepped outside for privacy.

Finally, on the fifth or sixth ring, Ben barked "H'lo?"

"Ben, it's Julia. I'm at Sandra Kempke's house. Her water just broke, she's got pain in her abdomen, she says she was vomiting earlier, and now she's saying something about lights. We got a problem."

She heard a muttered curse. "Yes we do. Get her over to the clinic. I'll call ahead and let InstaDoc know." Without further ado, he hung up the phone.

She walked back into the house. "We're taking you to the clinic," said Julia in as soothing a tone as she could manage. She even smiled at Sandra. Inside, though, a terrified high-pitched voice wailed *not again not this not again not again*, while her heart pounded and her palms grew damp with sweat.

The bundled Sandra into Todd's sheriff's car parked in the driveway. He put his flashing lights on and bombed into town toward the clinic. Julia followed in her car.

Ben was already there, looking thrown together and with damp hair, as if he'd been pulled out of the shower. Limping heavily, he was pulling a gurney out of the clinic with another man whom Julia assumed was InstaDoc. "Can you put her on this?"

Ben asked Todd, who nodded and gently lifted his wife onto the gurney. Dan Kendall strapped her on and covered her with a blanket. They pushed her into the clinic.

Sandra moaned at the bumpy ride, and her arms thrashed. "Make it stop, make it *stop*," she groaned.

"Make *what* stop, honey?" asked Todd.

"Make it stop," she whimpered, not hearing. Todd looked at Julia, terror in his face.

It was all she could do not to mirror the same emotion. She wanted to turn tail and run, to let Ben and Dan Kendall deal with this emergency. To run away and hide. To protect her herself. To not tear open another wound inside her...

****

Ben had a sinking feeling about Sandra Kempke, the same feeling he'd had from the start about her. That's why he wanted her safe at Gritman Medical Center in Moscow before there was any danger from premature labor. But this...this was too early!

They rolled the gurney into the operating room and transferred Sandra to the exam table. Todd clutched his wife's hand and talked to her. "Honey, you have to lie still, okay? Sandy? Can you hear me? Ben, why won't she lie still?"

"Seizures," snapped Ben. Sandra was shaking violently, her body rigid. "Get some magnesium sulfate ready, Julia—use the IV push. That'll prevent any more. Todd, either get out or get out of the way. Dan, call ahead to Moscow, tell them we've got a severe pre-eclamptic coming their way later tonight. They'll need a space in the NICU ready for the baby. Julia, do you have that IV ready? Julia? Julia!"

Julia stood stiff, the IV instruments in her hands, and stared at Sandra. She was pale as paper.

"Julia!" repeated Ben. What was wrong with her? Julia snapped to attention and, with shaking hands, tapped into the vein on Sandra's hand. She managed to slip the needle in and tape the IV to the skin.

As the magnesium sulfate began to flow into her body, Sandra stopped the violent shaking and appeared to be unconscious. Todd stepped forward, eyes like saucers. Then he glanced at Ben's grim face and stepped back again.

Dan Kendall came back in the room. "Moscow's all ready for her," he said. "Do you want a LifeFlight over?"

"Yes," said Ben. "But they'll have to take her afterward." He laid a hand on Sandra's abdomen. Everyone could see the wrenching contraction that grasped the woman's body. A moan was jerked from her lips, and she opened her eyes. "Todd..." she whispered.

"She's thirty-four weeks—prepare to C-section," said Ben. "It's the only way we're going to save this baby. Dan, get Moscow on the line, I want a constant link throughout in case we have further complications. Julia, check her blood pressure, then scrub up...Julia? *Julia!*"

What on earth was wrong with the woman? Julia continued to stare at Sandra with what looked like rigid terror. She seemed incapable of following the most basic orders. Ben had an irrational urge to slap her back to work.

She blinked at his order. "B-blood pressure?" she repeated.

"Yes. Now snap to it. I'm going to scrub."

Ben shooed the frantic Todd out of the room, then yanked on a sterile surgical gown and scrubbed his hands and arms. Dan came back in the room and did the same thing. Then they prepped Sandra for the C-section, using Povidone-iodine spray and the sterile tent.

"Dammit," muttered Ben, as he prepared for surgery, "I was afraid of this. I thought she had more time, though."

"I'll administer a general," said Dan. "Her condition is deteriorating. We need to get this baby out."

"Have you done generals before?" asked Ben.

"Yes."

"Thank God. I'm iffy on them. Go for it, man."

"What do you have—thiopental, methohexital, what?"

"Ketamine."

"Anything else? Ketamine shouldn't be used in pre-eclampsia."

"That's right. Damn, good thing you're here. We've got Diprivan."

Dan Kendall closed his eyes a moment and murmured, "Diprivan...two to three milligrams per kilogram, IV bolus..." Then he began inserting an 18-gauge catheter while Ben monitored the fetal heart rate. Dan fitted an oxygen mask over Sandra's face.

"Julia, I'll need you to take over monitoring the fetal heart rate," said Ben, while he yanked over a cart filled with surgical instruments.

When Julia didn't materialize to take over the monitor, he jerked his head around. "Julia?"

She was backed against a wall, staring with wild, hunted eyes, clearly terrified.

"Julia, get over here!"

She shook her head.

"Julia, *get over here now!*"

She shook her head again. Then to Ben's utter amazement, she gasped once, turned, and fled the room.

Both men stared after her, their patient momentarily forgotten.

"That's your *resident?*" asked Dan in amazement.

"Yeah."

"What's the matter with her?"

"Got me. Up until now she's been great." Ben turned his attention back to Sandra. "But one thing is certain—I sure as hell am going to get to the bottom of this as soon as Sandra's on her way to Gritman."

Ben made a horizontal rather than a vertical incision in Sandra's abdomen. The baby wasn't in any immediate danger, and he didn't want to scar Sandra any more than necessary.

With the cordless phone to his ear to the hospital in Moscow, Ben incised the skin and then the uterus as Dan stood by. When he laid open the uterus, Ben murmured, "There's my little darlin'." Dan suctioned out the amniotic fluid as Ben gently lifted the tiny boy from Sandra's uterus. Then Dan cut and clamped the umbilical cord and laid the baby on a warming table while Ben sucked mucus out of the baby's nose and mouth.

"Beautiful," said Dan.

"Yes. Apgar 6, I'd say. Good marks for his gestational age."

Dan took over care of the baby while Ben returned to Sandra. He removed the troublesome placenta, made sure Sandra's uterus was clean, and sutured her with dissolvable stitches. Then he sutured her skin, bandaged the wound, and made Sandra presentable. He thanked the consulting doctor in Moscow, told them that Sandra would be there shortly, and hung up.

"How the baby?" he asked Dan.

"Doing well."

"Go get Todd. He's probably wearing holes in the carpet."

Todd entered the room and his eyes darted

toward his unconscious wife.

"She's fine," said Ben, stripping off his gloves. "We'll airlift her to Gritman as soon as LifeFlight gets here. It was close, Todd."

Todd nodded, closed his eyes, and burst into tears.

Ben smiled and clapped the strong man on the shoulder. "You'll go with her to Moscow, okay? Hey, man...look at your son. He's doing great."

Todd sniffed and composed himself, then looked with awe at the tiny infant lying on the warmer. "Will he be okay?"

"He's doing fine. Got him out before uterine conditions deteriorated too much. He'll have to stay in the NICU at Gritman for awhile, and they'll monitor him closely. But he's a handsome little thing."

Todd sniffed again. "Thanks, Doc. Both of you." He looked around. "Where's Julia?"

****

Half an hour later, Ben and Dan watched the LifeFlight helicopter airlift Sandra, Todd, and their new baby son into the night sky, toward Moscow for post-natal care.

"Whew," Ben sighed, and slumped against a pole. "That's only the third time I've done an emergency C-section."

"You did great," said Dan warmly, and clapped Ben on the back. "Doesn't look like she'll be developing HELPP either." HELPP, Ben knew, was a post-eclampsia condition in which red blood cells break down, liver enzymes were elevated, and platelet count decreased.

"Close call, though."

"Yes," said Dan. "But she came through it better than I expected." He paused, and added, "Which is more than I can say for your resident."

Ben shook his head and thrust his hand through

his hair. "What in God's name got into her, I have no idea." His lips thinned. "I'm trying not to be furious enough to break her neck. Up until now she's had a cool head in an emergency. You should have seen her sew up a chain saw deep-wound trauma last week, tight as a drum. The injury was way beyond me, yet she handled it as if it were nothing. Why *this* would freak her, I have no idea."

"Makes me wonder if she'll stick it out through her residency," commented Dan. "Don't be too hard on her, though. Remember what it was like to be a resident? You don't know something, you freeze up."

"Oh sure. I've frozen up a few times—but I've never panicked and run from a room. I mean, she *panicked*, Dan. Just went to pieces. A doctor can't do that. What if she'd been alone with Sandra when this occurred?"

"Hmmm. Well, time will tell, I guess. How much longer does she have here?"

"Her three-month rotation is up at the end of June."

"You ought to sic her on all your other maternity patients as penance."

"Maybe I will."

"Ben, can you stay here for ten minutes while I walk over to the café and get a cappuccino?"

"Yeah, go ahead. I'll start to clean up in here."

Ben headed into the room where they'd done their emergency surgery. He was relieved that the outcome of Sandra's pregnancy was the survival of the baby...no help to Julia. He slammed his fist into the padded exam table. Why did she do it? Why did she panic like that?

He paused. In the deserted clinic, he heard a noise.

He followed it down the hall to the linen closet. From inside he heard the sound of frenzied weeping.

It could only be Julia. He'd thought she'd gone

104

home after her mad dash from the surgery, but it seemed she'd gone into hiding instead.

He yanked open the door.

She sat in the dark closet on a laundry bag stuffed with soiled linens, crying into a towel. When the light hit her, she jerked her face up and hiccupped. She looked, he thought uncharitably, terrible. Her eyes were swollen, her nose was red, her cheeks mottled.

"Would you like to explain what the hell happened back there?" he barked.

She buried her face in the towel once more and sobbed. He recognized the signs of impending hysteria and knew that anger at this moment would only push her over the edge.

He reached down, gripped her by the arm, and pulled her upright. "My place," he ordered. "Get going. You have some explaining to do."

She nodded and stumbled out of the closet. They came out of the clinic into the still night air, with crickets chirping in the grasses. Ben saw Dan walking back from the café with a large paper cup in hand. He waved, and Dan waved back.

Within five minutes, Ben had marched Julia to his house. She still clutched the towel and gave an occasional hiccup. Once inside the house, he pushed her toward the bathroom. "Go take a shower and calm down," he ordered. "Here's a clean robe." He yanked his spare bathrobe off its hook and tossed it at her. "Come out when you're ready to talk. And Julia...by God, it had better be good."

He turned his back on her and went into the kitchen, where he started to make coffee. He changed his mind, however, and poured two large glasses of wine instead. He brought the glasses and the bottle into the living room and set them on the coffee table.

He started a fire in the woodstove, more for the

companionable flames than for warmth. The light flickered around the room and threw shimmers of radiance on the walls of books. Sensing his mood, Gypsy didn't throw herself at him in her usual display of affection. Instead, she came and rested her head on his knee.

"What *happened* to her?" he asked the dog, stroking her head. "A doctor can't panic when faced with difficult cases." He leaned back and shut his eyes, suddenly tired. "This may not work out," he added. Whether he meant Julia's association with the clinic, or association with him, he couldn't say.

The bathroom door opened. Ben opened his eyes and watched Julia come out, clad in his large plaid bathrobe. Her face was scrubbed and clean, though her eyes were still red. Her hair was dry and still pinned up.

Ben's groin tightened at the sight of her, unclothed except for the robe. The anger and adrenaline from the evening's emergency now translated into a different channel. God, how he wanted to yank those damned pins from her hair and bury his face in it...

"Sit down," he ordered, and pointed to the sofa chair adjacent. "There's an extra-large glass of wine. I have a feeling you need it." He kept his tone stern and unsympathetic.

She gave a tug to the bathrobe tie and sat, then picked up the glass of wine and took a large gulp. Then, as he had done, she leaned her head back, closed her eyes, and sighed.

"Am I fired?" she asked.

"You deserve to be."

"I know."

He waited, but she didn't seem inclined to say anything more. Finally the precarious hold on his temper snapped. "Dammit, Julia, what the hell happened? Why did you panic?"

She raised her head and looked at him with hollow eyes. "I was reliving my past," she said quietly. "I lost a mother and baby to eclampsia last January."

Whatever he expected her to say, it wasn't this. The air whooshed out of his lungs as if he'd been hit. "Ouch."

"Yeah. Ouch." She took another gulp of the wine, and another.

"Okay, then...out with it. Tell me everything."

She leaned her head back against the sofa again, and he saw a tear leak out of the corner of one eye. But she spoke with an utterly emotionless voice.

"The mother had been living on the streets. She couldn't have been older than eighteen or nineteen. No prenatal care at all. We're estimating she was at thirty-four, thirty-five weeks, but had nothing precise, of course. She wandered into the ER having seizures. I was doing my ER rotation and was on duty..."

"Alone?"

"Skeletal staff. It was late at night, and a lot of the staff were working on three traumas from a bad car accident." She leaned forward and placed the glass of wine on the coffee table. "I was the only one who could be spared to help this girl. And no matter what I did...no matter what I did...she didn't make it." She shuddered and covered her face with her hands. "God, she was so young..."

Ben didn't move forward to offer any sympathy. He simply let her relive the worst parts. "What techniques did you use?"

"Everything, it seemed. Her blood pressure was sky high. She started having seizures, so I used magnesium sulfate to try and stop them. When that didn't work, I used Dilantin. She still had hypertension, so I tried Hydralazine. I was trying to monitor the fetus in the meantime, and it just seemed that that poor baby was severely distressed. And I couldn't do anything about it." She drew a sobbing breath. "I punched the emergency button, tried to get more staff to help me, but they had dying patients all over the place and no one could be spared."

Ben made a noise. "How can you triage when everyone's in the same boat?" he muttered.

"That's it exactly." She leaned forward and snagged the glass of wine, and took another large gulp. "And so it went. I finally realized that I had to get that baby out of her. I rushed her up to Obstetrics and had them alert the OB/GYN on call. But by then it was too late. She had heart failure and just died on me. I saw it all. And I couldn't help her. Couldn't help her..."

She sat slumped with her elbows on her knees, staring at her glass.

"Look," said Ben. "You have no idea what kind of pre-existing conditions she had. She could have had hypertension, or diabetes, or even a renal disease or a heart condition. But you're blaming yourself for her death even though it wasn't your fault."

"Don't you think I've told myself that over and over again?"

"We all lose patients, you know," said Ben gently.

"I know. That's what Alex told me."

He stiffened. "Alex, your ex-fiancé?"

"Yes." She gulped more wine and put the empty glass on the table.

Without hesitating, Ben reached over and filled the glass again. "So where does he come into this?"

Julia picked up the glass and fiddled with it, nearly spilling the contents. "I... well, I sort of fell apart after the woman died. And Alex—well, he couldn't handle it. He called me a wimp, a damn fool, all sorts of names. Basically, I was weak. He was strong. So he left me."

Ben felt a slow anger build inside him. To callously dump a fiancée was cruel at best. But to kick someone when they're down...

"Anyway," continued Julia, in the same dead monotone, "ever since then I've been scared to death about emergency maternity cases. And it's the pre-eclampsia that scares me most of all."

"That surprises me," said Ben.

She lifted her head. "Why?"

"Well, after you sewed up Jake Smothers, I was impressed as hell. I'd never seen a GP handle that kind of emergency so well, Julia—and that's the truth. If I'd been there alone, the best I could have done was to stop the bleeding and get him to Moscow. But you saved his arm."

"But that was easy, compared to—"

"No, it *wasn't* easy," he snapped. "And maybe that's where the problem is. You handled that case so well—as you have everything, so far—that I extrapolated too much. I assumed you would handle *everything* with the same degree of skill. My mistake."

"*You* didn't know I had this phobia!"

"No, and *you* didn't tell me about it, despite the fact that you knew Sandra was pre-eclamptic. And *that's* what pisses me off more than anything else— you put *her* life in danger by not telling me about *your* little problem."

"I know." She ran a hand over her forehead.

"So here's what you're going to do." Ben leaned forward to emphasize his words. "As you know, Sandra's twin sister Sara is also pre-eclamptic. From now on, Sara is yours. You will deal entirely with her pregnancy. You will be prepared to handle her if a similar emergency occurs. You will *not* panic because you'll be so ready for anything that you could do an emergency C-section in your sleep."

He saw fear spring to her eyes, but she only set her lips. "That's fair. Then this is what I ask in return: drill me on everything. Any possible contingency associated the pre-eclamptics, drill me. Call me in the middle of the night and give me a pop quiz, if you have to. That's the only way I'll be able to overcome this dread I have."

Ben nodded, impressed. "Fair enough. Okay, the lecture's over." He felt the tension leave him, and realized it was because—despite her blunder tonight—he trusted her to handle herself professionally as a doctor. "Tomorrow you'll start your education in handling Sara."

"I thought tomorrow was a day off."

"For me, maybe. For you...well, I suggest you go to the clinic and meet Dan Kendall properly. Apologize and tell him about our arrangement. Then take home a few of the texts we have at the clinic and spend your weekend memorizing dosages and techniques and even the phone number to Gritman."

"So much for sightseeing."

"Yes. So much for sightseeing. You have more important things to do."

She nodded again and took another sip of wine, then held her glass out. "It's almost empty," she said with surprise. "Ben, how much wine did you give me?"

"Enough to make you tipsy," he answered. He leaned forward, lifted the wine bottle off the table, and filled her glass a third time. "There are times when a little alcohol can be useful. You needed to relax."

"If I relax any more, I'll be drunk." She accepted the refill and leaned back. The top of the bathrobe gapped open a bit, revealing a shadowed cleft. Instantly Ben's thoughts drifted southward, and his body tightened.

"Maybe you'd better go home now," he muttered.

She looked at him. "Why?"

"Because suddenly I'm having prurient thoughts about you, imagining what's underneath that bathrobe."

She glanced down at the robe and yanked the tie tighter. "Oh."

"Yes. Oh. Julia, do you have idea what you do to me?"

She bit her lip. "I've wondered."

He gave a short, humorless laugh. "Wondered about what? About my dragging you off to bed and making violent love to you?"

"Yes."

The simple word caused his thoughts to tumble and his body to react even more. "Damn," he groaned.

"Ben, if that's what's been on your mind, why haven't you done anything about it?"

He stared at her. "You mean, drag you off to bed? Don't tempt me."

She leaned over and placed her wineglass on the table. Then, to his considerable surprise, she slid over onto the sofa with him and curled up against his chest. "Who's tempting whom?"

"Julia, don't," he groaned. His body was ramrod stiff. "I'm only human."

"Me too." She reached up and yanked out four hairpins, then shook her head so that the black mass cascaded free. "So do something about it."

Still he held himself back, though the urge to thrust his hands into that erotic hair nearly blinded him. "Julia..."

"Look, if you don't make the first move, I will." She placed her hands on either side of his face and fused her lips to his.

He tried to control himself, he really did. He kept his hands to himself. He didn't deepen the kiss. He made sure...

"Kiss me, Ben," she murmured, and touched him intimately.

His control snapped. He pushed inside the bathrobe and felt her breasts, full and warm, fall into his hands. She moved until she straddled him, still linked by the kiss. And that marvelous hair swept over them like a curtain.

Within moments Ben couldn't stand it any longer. He stood up and dragged her into his arms, lifted her off her feet, and carried her into the bedroom. When he laid her on the bed, the robe fell half-open, and in the dim light spilling from the living room he saw the flawless, rosy skin beckon him. "God, you're gorgeous," he whispered, and stripped off his clothes before she could change her mind. Then he fell on the bed with her and plunged his hand into the robe again.

After a moment he slowed and stopped. "I can't do this," he muttered. "You're drunk, and I would be taking advantage of you."

"I'm *not* drunk. And *I'm* the one egging you on."

"Can't do it," he gritted. "Wouldn't be right..."

"Will you shut up and make love to me?" Julia reached up and yanked him down to her level. "I'm tired of waiting."

Ben knew he was lost. "It'll be worth the wait," he said. Trailing a finger down from breast to waist and below, he felt her body tremble. She reached over and stroked him, jerking a groan from his lips. "Julia, it's been a long time...I don't know if I can control myself for long..."

"Then don't wait any longer," she whispered. She yanked open the bathrobe tie and pulled him on top of her.

Blindly, like a mindless animal, Ben thrust home and growled with pleasure as he sank into her depths. She wrapped her legs around him, urging him on without apparent care for her own

112

satisfaction

Ben had never before felt a rush of lust grip him so powerfully. He plunged into her like a wild thing, thrusting his hands into her hair and feeling the press of her breasts against his chest. For long minutes they thrust together, beating, pounding, pulsing in a perfect cadence.

Then he lost all control, bucking into her until with a wild shout that tore her mouth from his, he shot over the edge of the cliff and poured himself into her.

Chapter Seven

Julia spent the night at Ben's house. Twice more they made love, slower and more satiating than that first wild tumble, and Julia knew Ben was happy when she took her own pleasure.

She lay across Ben's chest and listened to his quiet breathing as he slept. The late night ticked toward morning. Her body felt full and content in the afterglow of sex. But while her body was happy, her mind was not.

She was ashamed of her behavior with Sandra—panicking and fleeing the scene. She was grateful that Todd was out of the room by then, and that Sandra was unconscious.

But something was different about this. Despite her panic and desertion when Ben needed her, he hadn't reacted with disgust and condemnation. He had been stern, yes; and firm about how she could redeem herself.

And he hadn't walked out on her. Strange. Instead, somehow, they miraculously ended up in bed together.

She felt relieved that Ben had trusted her enough to continue her training... because becoming a full-fledged doctor was the only thing she could count on.

She snuggled closer to Ben, wrapping her arm around his waist. *Don't cling, Julia*, she reminded herself. *It won't change anything. It won't last.* Nothing in her life ever did, except education.

Her medical training would last. Ben would not.

That was a fact. When her rotation was up, she would leave Jasper and go back to Portland. She would leave Ben... before he left her.

But not yet.

****

Julia sat on Ben's living room floor, with her back against the base of the sofa and medical texts strewn around her. Ben sat on the couch reading a book. Every so often he reached a hand down and caressed a strand of her hair, which Julia had left down.

"You have a hair fetish," she commented at one point.

"Hmmm—maybe I do. But there's just something so erotic about a woman with long hair."

She turned her head and dropped a kiss on his hand before returning to her books.

"A vertical incision on the uterus causes less bleeding and better access to the fetus, but renders the mother unable to attempt a vaginal delivery in the future..." she murmured.

"Yes," said Ben. "The reason is that patients with vertical uterine incisions have a much higher chance of rupturing the uterus in the future pregnancies, compared to those with horizontal incisions. That's why I did a horizontal incision on Sandra, both on her abdomen and her uterus. The baby wasn't in any immediate distress, so I had that option."

"...cut open the amniotic sac, and allow the fluid to drain—did you do that, or Dan Kendall?"

"Dan. He sucked the fluid out while I lifted up the baby. You hold the baby's head with one hand, and sort of gently push on the uterus with the other to get the baby out. It's a little different with a vertical incision—then you can just sort of scoop the kid up. But because you don't have complete access with a horizontal incision, you need to support the head while you push the baby out."

"Yes, I've done that."

"Oh, so you *have* done C-sections before?"

"Yes. But not emergency ones."

"You'll do fine when Sara has her baby," he told her. "Even if it goes as badly as Sandra's."

Julia took a deep breath and let it out again. "I appreciate the vote of confidence, but I don't feel as optimistic as you do. That's why I can't take chances on this." She glanced over at him. "Your idea is a good one—to put me in charge of Sara. I'm so frantic to prove myself that it's like I'm in medical school again."

"Whatever it takes. It could be, literally, a life or death issue. Neither of us can take chances. And if you flub it up, I'll be right there to step in and take over. I trust you, Julia, but not at the expense of Sara's life, or the life of her baby."

She set her mouth. "I won't let you down, Ben. You, or Sara…or me."

From his position on the couch, he tipped her head back and laid a long, lingering kiss on her lips. His hand snaked down inside her shirt and gently caressed one breast. Julia felt the heat bubble up in her system.

"I can't spend the night again, you know," she murmured.

"Why not?"

"People will talk. This is a small town. Everyone's business is public knowledge. Besides, I have to go home and feed the cat."

Ben's hand tightened. "Then we'd better make hay while the sun shines."

****

"There's nothing like a little physical therapy," gritted Ben, "to reduce the libido to nothing." He grunted as Julia moved his leg in the hip socket.

"The sooner you get this done with, the sooner

116

your libido will return," said Julia. She completed the exercise and let Ben rest a moment. Sweat had popped out on his forehead at the painful moves. "You're getting better, though. Even after a week, I can see the progress."

"I went out to get the mail yesterday without my cane," he bragged. "First time."

"Not bad." She grinned at him. "Within two weeks, I'll have to run to get away from you."

"Don't run too fast. I want to be able to catch you."

****

"You're like a fever in my blood," she murmured in the aftermath of a particularly stimulating session of lovemaking.

"That makes two of us," he said. He cupped a breast and kissed the tip. "Of course, *I* knew that from the start. *You* just figured it out."

"True." She sighed and laid a hand on his chest, feeling his heartbeat coming back to normal. "I was so weighed down with guilt and pain, both from losing the patient and from Alex walking out on me."

"Julia..." Ben captured one of her hands. "What about that rotation in internal medicine that he arranged for you? What are you going to do about it?"

Her euphoria dimmed. "I don't know. I may not have much choice but to take it. And...and..." She bit her lip. "And I'm still anxious to return to the city," she finished, low.

She felt Ben stiffen. Though he didn't say anything, the intimacy between them fled.

"I have to go, Ben," she said quietly. "You knew that from the beginning."

He rolled off the bed and started pulling on his clothes. "It's so damn difficult to attract doctors to this town," he said bitterly. "And women too."

Julie sat up and clutched the sheet to her bare

breasts. "You knew from the start that this was temporary."

"Oh yeah. You made that perfectly clear. A punishment. An exile." He sat on the bed and thrust a hand through his hair. "I guess I read too much into your lovemaking. You make a man forget everything, Julia. Common sense. Rational thought." He reached out and lifted a heavy strand of her hair, running his fingers over it and lifting it over her shoulder, where it rested on the rise of one breast under the sheet. "But I'm going to spend the rest of your time here convincing you to change your mind."

****

On Monday, before InstaDoc left to go to his next circuit, Ben and Julia drove up to Moscow to see Sandra.

"I have a favor to ask," said Julia. She gripped her hands between her knees and looked at the road ahead.

She could feel Ben glance at her as he held the steering wheel. "Okay."

"Please don't tell Sandra about my... well, my mess-up last Thursday. She was pretty out of it, and I don't think she knows how badly I blew it."

"Don't worry, I won't tell her," he said. "But not for the reason you think. My reasoning is that she's close to her twin, Sara. Since you'll be entirely taking over Sara's care, I don't want anything negative to get back to her and make her less confident in your ability to handle her."

"Well, that's an aspect I hadn't considered," admitted Julia.

"Speaking of which, why don't you want to use ketamine under emergency C-section conditions?"

"Well, for one, ketamine doesn't provide muscular relaxation, so the incision may need to be longer. Plus it's more dangerous for women with high-blood pressure and pre-eclamptics."

"Good. How about if a patient is having seizures? What do you do?"

"Administer magnesium sulfate intravenously."

"And if that doesn't stop the seizures?"

"Then use..." Julia paused for a second, thinking. "Benzodiazepine or phenytoin."

"Good. You're getting there."

They drove to Gritman Medical Center. Sandra looked much better. She sat up with a smile in the hospital bed. "Hi!"

"Came to see how you're doing," said Ben, while Julia hung back.

"Much better. The doctor said I'm out of danger and the baby and I should be going home next week."

"What did you name the baby?"

"Aaron. It means 'exulted.' Because it's a miracle he's here." Sandra paused and added shyly, "Thanks entirely to you two."

Julia was grateful that Ben did nothing more than graciously accept Sandra's thanks without implicating her in any misconduct. Julia was so deeply ashamed that she could hardly even admire little Aaron when Sandra had a nurse wheel in his little incubator.

"Would you like to hold him?" Sandra asked Julia.

She hardly dared admit how much she wished to. "Yes." The baby was tiny, but he felt so blessedly *alive* to her as she lifted him up and cuddled him. "He's beautiful, Sandra."

"Todd is so happy he can hardly tear himself away from here to go to work." Sandra smiled. "And I still can't believe he's here. My little miracle baby." She sniffed and wiped her eyes.

Julia felt her own eyes moisten. She transferred the infant into Sandra's arms, and without shame Sandra bared a breast and guided the tiny lips toward the nourishment. The newborn latched on with surprising vigor.

Julia felt another sting of emotion. Sandra—wan and bruised after her trial—was beautiful as she bonded with her baby.

"You did that on purpose, didn't you?" asked Julia on the way home.

"Did what?"

"Bringing me in to see Sandra. To show me how a successful handling of a pre-eclamptic emergency can turn out."

He grinned. "Did it motivate you?"

"Like you wouldn't believe."

"Then I succeeded in my mission."

"She was beautiful, wasn't she?" Julia's eyes turned inward. "Sandra looked like a cement truck had rolled over her, yet as she lay there in her hospital bed nursing her baby, she looked...well, beautiful."

Ben glanced her way. "Envious?"

Julia signed. "Maybe just a little."

****

The phone rang, shattering Julia's sleep. Grunting, she groped for the telephone as she saw the glowing dial on the clock that said 2:25. "H'lo?"

"What do you *not* suture closed when finishing up an emergency C-section?" said Ben's voice.

Despite her muddled brain, Julia couldn't help but smile. "Boy, you're serious about this, aren't you?"

"Yes. So what don't you suture? And why?"

"You don't suture shut the peritoneum, because it heals up on its own, and sutures might cause adhesions in the future. And you don't suture the abdominal muscles—you just tie them loosely with dissolvable stitches."

"Good. G'night, Julia."

"Good night." Julia hung up the phone and lay

back in bed, grinning.

****

"It's beautiful out today. Let's go hit the lake after work."

Julia looked up from a file on her desk. "And do what?"

"I don't know. Walk. Fish. Sit on the dock and dangle our feet in the water. Swim..."

"Swim? Don't you think it's too cold?"

He grinned at her. "Yes. But I was looking for an excuse to see you in a bathing suit."

"Shhhh....Ben, someone might hear you."

"They're going to find out eventually. It's not like I'm ashamed to be seen with you, Julia."

"No, but nor do we have to advertise ourselves in front of your staff." She smiled. "But that's fine with me. Hitting the lake, that is. Are there any walking trails?"

"Tons. Got any hiking boots?"

"No. Will sneakers work?"

"They should. Good. It's a date, then. Meanwhile, guess what—Sara Johanson is here for her weekly appointment."

Feeling butterflies in her stomach, Julia rose. "Does she know I'm taking over her case?"

"Not yet. Do you want me to go in with you and explain?"

"No. I'll do it, unless she wants to talk to you afterward."

"Here's her file, then."

Ben handed her Sara's paperwork, and Julia tucked it under her arm and walked down the hall to the exam room where Sara waited.

"Hello, Sara," she said, walking into the room and closing the door behind her. "How are you feeling?"

"Pretty tired," said Sara. She was already attired in an examination robe. Her face was puffy and she had dark circles under her eyes. "But I'm surviving."

"I'll be taking over your prenatal care from now on," said Julia. "All your future appointments will be with me, unless I'm unavailable. Is that all right with you?

"Are you kidding? I'd love it!"

Sara's enthusiasm was flattering. Julia managed a chuckle. "I seem to remember your sister saying something about Ben being good, but there was some relief in knowing that the doctor looking at her private parts is *not* the same person who pulled her hair in fourth grade." She helped Sara lie on the exam table.

"That sounds like Sandra." Sara smiled. "Always the fighter."

Thank God for that, thought Julia. "Are you a fighter too?"

"Not really. Sandra got all the feisty genes in the family."

It was ridiculous to take such a trivial comment and blow it all out of proportion. But Julia couldn't shake the chill as she gave Sara a thorough checkup. "Have you already given your urine sample to Adele?"

"Yes."

"She'll check it for protein and sugar content. It's pretty obvious you're pre-eclamptic. I'm sure Ben has emphasized how important it is to take care of yourself, especially since you lost your last baby."

"Yes. And after Sandra's drama last week..." Sara bit her lip, and Julia saw unshed tears sparkle in her eyes. "It's pretty scary, to almost lose your twin."

"I can imagine. But she's fine, and so is her baby. And you'll be fine, too. Try not to dwell on the negative, okay?" *If only I could follow my own advice*, thought Julia.

"Okay." Sara gave a sign and wiped her eye. "I trust you, Julia. And I'm thankful you're here."

Guilt lanced through her. *I trust you, Julia...*If only she was worthy of that trust.

Sara was the last appointment of the day. Ben and Julia closed up the clinic, and Julia agreed to meet Ben at his house after she'd changed her clothes.

"Now admit it," said Ben, as he drove toward Lake Percheron. "This place is looking nicer now that summer is only here."

"Okay, I'll admit it. And I'll also admit that I've never seen a place with so many wildflowers. What are those over there?"

"Arnica. I'll point out the plants as we see them on the trail."

The hiking trail skirted the lake and was nothing short of beautiful. Ben pointed out the local wildflowers blooming at the moment: wild roses, salsify, yarrow, trumpet honeysuckle, vetch, lupine. They made a pretty contrast to the blue water and the blue sky and the dark green conifers. Birds sang in profusion, and the afternoon sun was warm. Julia sighed. "This sure eases problems from work."

"What problems?"

"Oh, Sara Johanson. She has me worried."

"Are you worried about *her*, or are you worried about *you?*"

"Both." Julia stopped on the trail and touched a blue flower with the toe of her sneaker.

"Don't let it stress you. You've been good about studying up on all possible contingencies so far. Likely Sara won't hit any problems until after her thirty-seventh week, when she'll be in Moscow and near Gritman Medical Center anyway. But if an emergency does arise, I'll be right here to support you. You'll do fine."

Julia knew his words were meant to comfort,

but it didn't relieve the clenched-fist sensation in the pit of her stomach. She rubbed her belly. "All this stress is going to give me an ulcer."

"Now Julia, you know that the latest research shows that ulcers are caused by bacteria, not stress."

"Easy for you to say. It's not *your* stomach that's hurting."

"Come on. Let's walk a bit and just enjoy the view." He took her hand, and swinging it gently they walked up the trail.

His prescription worked. The beautiful scenery, the sweet fresh air, the simple companionship of walking along an outdoor trail holding hands...Julia wanted it to go on forever.

Amid such beauty, Ben stopped and turned to face her. He lifted their clasped hands and dropped a kiss on her knuckles. "What are some techniques for managing post-partum hemorrhaging?"

Julia burst out laughing. "Be still, my heart. Oh Ben, you romantic thing you."

He grinned. "So what's the answer?"

Julia turned and continued walking. "Assuming a vaginal delivery, I'd recommend administering oxytocin right after the baby is delivered. Get the cord clamped and cut as soon as possible. Then do a Brandt-Andrews maneuver—a gentle cord traction with uterine countertraction."

"Hmmm—good. Very good. You must have aced your exams."

"Didn't do too badly." She smiled.

His hand tightened around hers. "Spend the night with me tonight?"

She felt a thrill go through her. "Maybe we should wait until the weekend."

"Why?"

She smiled. "You're right. Why not? Okay. I'll come over after dinner."

"Why don't you come over and *have* dinner?

Then you can stay."

"I have to make sure I feed the cat."

"Then feed him and come over. Did you ever name him, by the way?"

"No." Her smile faded.

"Why not?"

"Because he's only temporary. I doubt I'll ever see him again after I'm gone."

"Running away again?"

"Not yet." She sighed.

****

On a Tuesday afternoon, Ben was in his office at the clinic, writing up a patient report. Gypsy snored at his feet. Julia was out, having gone to do a follow-up call on Jake Smothers.

Lisa, the receptionist, buzzed his phone. "Ben, there's a Dr. Pat Schweitzer on line one for you."

"Thanks." Ben picked up the phone. "This is Dr. Ben Taylor."

"Good afternoon, Dr. Taylor," said a man's voice. "My name is Pat Schweitzer. I'm the medical director for the Residency Program here at Portland City Hospital."

"Nice to meet you, Dr. Schweitzer," said Ben. "Are you calling about Julia?"

"Yes. I thought I'd see how she's working out for you."

Ben leaned back in is desk chair, conflicted. "Truthfully?"

There was a pause at the other end of the line. "Yes, of course truthfully."

Ben ran a hand through his hair. Professionally he knew he was doing the right thing. But personally—personally, he felt he was betraying Julia. "In many ways, Dr. Schweitzer, she has far surpassed our expectations." He related the incident with Jake Smothers' arm wound. "She beat me on that one. I'd never addressed such a severe trauma, and yet she handled it as if she'd done it dozens of times. And yet..."

"And yet?" prompted Dr. Schweitzer.

Ben sighed. "We had a pre-eclamptic patient who went into premature labor a couple of weeks ago. Julia was with her when the patient's water broke, and whisked her into the clinic. We had no time to get her to the regional hospital—our circuit doctor and I had to do an emergency C-section. And Julia—well, Dr. Schweitzer, she froze up. Simply panicked. I needed her to take over monitoring the fetal heart rate, and she literally ran from the room. Later I found her crying hysterically. It came out that she was traumatized from losing a pre-eclamptic patient when she was doing her ER rotation. She admitted to something approaching a phobia when it came to those kinds of cases."

"I knew she was upset when she lost that patient," said Schweitzer thoughtfully. "But I had no idea that it had developed into a phobia. That's certainly not acceptable behavior for a doctor."

"I agree, it's not," said Ben. "Oddly enough, however, she'll have an opportunity to redeem herself. The pre-eclamptic patient has a twin sister who is also pregnant and also pre-eclamptic. Now, the odds are excellent that this woman will hang on until her thirty-seventh week, when she'll take up residence close to the regional hospital, which has an excellent NICU. However, for the time being I've put Julia completely in charge of this patient's care. Also, I'm having her study up on all possible emergency contingencies that might occur—popping quizzes at her, pushing textbooks at her. She's been very diligent about this, I'm sure due to some remorse."

"That's a good idea."

"That's what I thought. So we'll see how she does with this patient. In light of her skill with the trauma wound, and her skills with all other aspects of medicine, I have hopes she'll handle this toxemia patient well. Besides, I'll be there at all times, and will intervene if she freezes up again."

"So overall you're satisfied with her performance?"

"Oh, very," replied Ben. *You have no idea how much*, he thought. "Her training here has been superb—perhaps not as intense or high-pressure as she might get in a city hospital, but because of our rural location we are called upon to deal with a much wider spectrum of cases, since there are no specialists to call upon. Unless we send the patient on to the hospital in Moscow, seventy miles away, that is."

"Now *that's* what I wanted to hear," said Schweitzer warmly. "I had a feeling that her training would be excellent in such a facility."

"Now, about her next rotation..." began Ben.

"Yes, there's an internist here who is interested in having her."

"Yes, that's what I heard. However, I would like to consider having her stay on here as long as she can, and possibly complete the rest of her residency here. We're a mixed bag of cases, but as you pointed out, the overall the training is excellent. And frankly, Dr. Schweitzer, it's hard to attract doctors to this area. It's been a relief to have someone else to share the workload."

"You're in a wheelchair for the time being, aren't you?"

"Not any more. I'm back on my feet, more or less, but I'm undergoing physical therapy three days a week, and I'm still in some pain and have limited mobility."

"Hmmm. It's certainly worth considering. As a Senior Resident, though, ultimately the decision is up to Julia, of course," replied Schweitzer.

Hope flared in Ben. "Of course."

"Well, I'll let you get back to work," said Dr. Schweitzer. "I'm pleased to know Julia is conducting herself professionally, with that one exception. Please keep me informed as to her progress."

"I will. And doctor—thank you. If Julia can stay on and complete her residency here, that would be of great help to this community." *And me,* thought Ben as he hung up.

Chapter Eight

Julia paused and looked out the window of her office in the clinic late on a Thursday afternoon. It had been four weeks since she and Ben had come together intimately. Four wonderful, sensual, incredible weeks.

She was rather proud of herself, really. She'd managed to keep herself emotionally at a distance...enough that, when she left to return to Portland, she wouldn't be leaving any of her heart here in Jasper with Ben.

She wondered if Ben suspected how detached she was determined to remain. If he knew that he didn't have the "whole" woman when they made love.

At least she hadn't made any more medical blunders since the night Sandra had her baby. Julia had studied—and Ben had quizzed her and tested her and interrogated her—on all possible aspects of Sara's condition until she could repeat things backward and forward.

"Watch," she'd told him the previous afternoon. "Sara won't have any problems. We'll whisk her off to Moscow in plenty of time, she'll sail her way through the end of her pregnancy, and come home with a healthy baby."

"Probably. But on the other hand, you'll never have a problem facing pre-eclamptic patients again," said Ben.

Remembering his words, Julia felt a chill go through her despite the beautiful early summer afternoon. His words had denoted the future...and the future was something Julia was thinking about more and more.

Her window faced the main street through Jasper. Though summer had arrived and beautified the region, as Ben had promised, she found herself missing Portland.

Starbucks. Department stores. The river. Museums. Everything.

She sighed and leaned on the windowsill, watching a robin out on the lawn hop around looking for worms. She'd been in Jasper for over two months now. She had to admit that she liked it better than she thought she would, but there was something special about the hustle and bustle of the city that she yearned for.

"Penny for your thoughts," said Ben from behind her.

She jerked around. "Oh! You startled me!"

"What were you thinking about?"

She dropped her eyes. "I was thinking about how much I missed Portland."

His mouth tightened. "I see."

"I'm sorry, Ben, but you *did* ask. I guess I'm just a city girl at heart."

"I think you're more a small-town girl who just doesn't want to admit it."

"And *I* think you're just saying that to convince me to stay."

"You could be right." He ran a hand through his hair. "You can't blame me for trying."

"No, I can't." Julia turned and dropped into her desk chair. "So what's up?"

"Remember I mentioned that there seemed to be some cases of whooping cough cropping up in Moscow?"

"Yes."

"Seems we have a case here, too."

"Oh no! That means it'll spread like wildfire around whoever isn't vaccinated."

"And now guess who's coming into the clinic."

"Who?"

"Retta Doyle."

Julia clearly remembered the hostility of the woman who refused to have her children vaccinated. "Who's sick?"

"Tyler. He's the four-year-old."

"And she's actually allowing him to be treated?" Julia was able to keep most of the sarcasm from her voice.

"The kid's sick as a dog. I strongly suspect it's whooping cough, though we'll have to see him to be sure, of course. If that's what he has, I'm just waiting for the others to come down with it."

"And Mrs. Doyle is pregnant, too."

"Yes."

"Oh joy." Julia rose. "Okay, let's go deal with the patient. Poor kid."

"There are no other appointments at the moment, which is a good thing. We'll both talk with her."

Lisa ushered Mrs. Doyle and Tyler into the exam room. Ben followed and lifted little Tyler onto the exam table and looked him over. He was fairly easy to diagnose, especially after he began coughing and gagging, and his lips took on a bluish tinge.

"I thought it was just a bad cold," said Retta Doyle, wringing her hands. "But it isn't getting better."

Julia supported the child until he finally stopped coughing and slumped, exhausted, into her arms. "Tyler, honey, I'd like you to open your mouth wide," she told him. "I need to put this little stick into your mouth and scrape just a bit at the back of your throat."

Tyler tried to open his mouth, but the action

bought on another horrible coughing fit. Julia managed to swab his throat before he got too bad. She dabbed the mucus onto a lab plate, and handed it to Ben. He left the room to begin culturing the sample.

"We'll culture the mucus just to make sure," said Julia, "but I think we can pretty much guarantee he has whooping cough."

The mother's face was drawn into lines of fear. "But I thought you couldn't get that disease around here! That it was no longer around!"

Julia was too angry to be diplomatic. "I told you earlier that there are always dormant populations of dangerous diseases, waiting to strike the unprepared. Now your son has whooping cough, and your other children stand a good chance of getting it too. What's next? Polio? Are you willing to risk having your children paralyzed because of your misinformation about vaccines?"

Mrs. Doyle turned pale, but Julia didn't care. She turned toward the boy. "I'd like to keep Tyler here at least overnight," she continued. "He has a long road of care ahead of him, and you'll need to learn what to do to minimize his coughing."

"Is...is he in any danger?"

Julia whirled on her. "*Yes*, he's in danger! Especially in small children, the coughing is so strong that oxygen levels are decreased—that's why his lips are turning blue. The force of the coughs could bring on seizures or hernias. It's a serious disease, Mrs. Doyle. *This* is what you risked by your refusal to vaccinate!"

The other woman staggered back, put her hands over her face, and burst into tears.

Julia felt remorse. Ben had remonstrated with her once about badgering patients, and Retta Doyle was pregnant and doubtless more emotional than usual. "Look, I'm sorry," she said, and drew the distraught woman into her arms. Mrs. Doyle leaned into Julia for a few moments and wept.

When she grew more composed, Julia handed her some tissues and sat her down. "I'm sorry I yelled, Mrs. Doyle. It's just that I see red when people don't understand the nature of vaccinations, and how dangerous the actual diseases are. We've grown so complacent in this country about being in no danger from infectious diseases. People don't remember what it was like to lose children to things like polio or smallpox or...or..." She avoided mentioning whooping cough. "...or other diseases. But now you need to consider your other children too."

Ben came back into the room. Retta Doyle turned to him in tears. "Ben, are my other kids in danger? Tell me I don't have to get them vaccinated."

He crossed his arms on his chest. "I've been telling you for years, Retta, that you're risking these diseases. Everyone in your household should be given erythromycin to reduce their chances of a serious whooping cough attack, though it's likely you'll all get it. The erythromycin won't help Tyler much, but it may keep the other kids from getting it as badly. And Retta—if there's any time to reconsider vaccinating your children at least against polio, it's now. Dr. Chambers is right to try to convince you."

Retta Doyle slumped in her chair. "I'll talk it over with Mike tonight," she said in a dull voice. She looked at Tyler, who lay exhausted on the exam table, his eyes closed. "Are you sure you have to keep him here tonight?"

"Yes," said Ben. "I want to monitor him for one night and see how he does. Then we'll give you very specific instructions for his care at home."

She nodded and rose to give Tyler a kiss. "Mommy has to leave you here, honey. These nice

133

people are going to take care of you, okay?"

Tyler started to cry, and the crying brought on another coughing fit. Retta Doyle bit her lip, turned, and left the room.

Julia held Tyler until the coughing subsided, then gave him his dose of erythromycin before tucking him into the one bed the clinic had for overnight patients. "I'll stay with him tonight," she told Ben. "I think a mild sedative might help him sleep better."

"I'll relieve you early," said Ben. "Around three a.m. or so. Call me if he gets worse."

The clinic gradually emptied of staff and patients. Julia pulled all her textbooks into Tyler's room and sat at the little desk in the room, continuing her studies on pre-eclampsia. Periodically Tyler would erupt into horrible, wracking coughs. Julia helped him through the fits, monitoring him to make sure he wasn't breaking any ribs from the strength of the coughing.

Around eight o'clock in the evening, she heard the small bell ring over the front door as it opened. Stepping into the hall, she saw Ben come into the clinic holding a small pizza box in one hand, and Gypsy's leash in the other. He was limping but didn't have his cane. He hadn't used it for a week now.

"How's Tyler?" he asked as he put the box on the desk in his office.

"Better. The sedative helped. He's mostly sleeping."

Ben checked on Tyler and nodded. "He'll do a little better with the erythromycin. It won't stop the cough, but it may lessen its severity."

"Ben, I have a confession to make. I...well, I yelled at Retta Doyle about her stubbornness in not vaccinating."

"Ah, such a wonderful bedside manner."

134

"It's not funny. I'm feeling guilty as anything over it."

"Then learn from your mistake. But if it makes you feel any better, you're not the only one. I've yelled at a few patients in my time."

Relief flooded her. "Really?"

"Really. We have a lot of stubborn people around here, and I guess you can count me as one of them." He shifted the pizza box in his hand.

"I see you brought dinner," said Julia, nodding toward the box.

"Yep. Come into my office—let's let Tyler sleep."

There was something intimate about being in Ben's office at night. Gypsy curled up in her accustomed spot. The desk lamps gave the room a warm, cozy glow. The books, the rustic prints on the walls, the colorful Turkish carpet, and the darkened windows, all created a homey atmosphere.

She could almost imagine, thought Julia, that it was hers and Ben's son lying in the next room. She shied away from the thought.

"Retta Doyle's pretty upset about all this," she commented, lifting a slice of pizza from the box.

"Maybe this will bring her and Mike around," replied Ben. "I've been after them since we had a measles outbreak around here a few years ago. Their kids escaped infection, and ever since then she's been gloating about how vaccinations are a waste of time and money, and dangerous to boot." He bit into some pizza. "Maybe this will change her mind."

"Maybe."

"How about you? Changed your mind yet?"

Startled, she stared at him. "About what?"

"About staying on here."

"Oh. That."

She saw him mouth compress. "Yes. That."

"I can't, Ben. Really I can't."

"I don't understand you, Julia. Isn't what we

135

share important to you?"

She began to feel trapped. "What we're sharing is sex, Ben. Nothing more, nothing less."

"I thought that was supposed to be the man's perspective. It's usually the woman who's looking for something more."

"Then that's your first mistake. You know I'm temporary here. I didn't come here looking for a relationship..."

"But you found it, didn't you?" Ben dropped a crust into the box, then changed his mind and gave it to the dog. "And now you're running scared. I never took you for a coward, Julia."

"I'm *not* a coward!"

"Oh yeah? Then how come every time I bring up the future, you back off and change the subject?"

She shook her head. "I thought you just came in to share a pizza with me. When did things become so complicated?"

"Every time you deny yourself, you're complicating things."

"Ben, I wish you would stop pressuring me. Whenever you start on this subject, it's like you're bullying me, and I won't put up with it."

His eyes cooled. "You're being foolish, Julia. You'll run back to Portland and do your rotation under your ex-fiancé who will squash you under your thumb like you're nothing. Is that what you want?"

"Ben, I said *drop* it."

"Fine. I will—for now." He stood up. "Good night, Julia. I'll be here around 3 a.m. to take over Tyler."

He took Gypsy's leash and walked out of the building. Slowly Julia got up and locked the clinic doors behind him.

Every time you deny yourself, you're complicating things...

Oh great. Now she would have Ben's voice

136

echoing in her ears. Even absent, he could pressure her.

Every time you deny yourself...

Knock it off, Julia, she told herself, and marched into Tyler's room to check on the little boy. *Denial is good. It's a survival mechanism. A rock feels no pain, and an island never cries.*

She dozed by Tyler's bedside, waking whenever the child had his coughing frenzies. His condition remained stable, however, and Julia thought that if the Doyle's continued the antibiotics, he might come through the disease without any secondary complications such as ear infections or pneumonia.

Deep into the night, a noise woke Julia. Jerking upright, she looked at Tyler, but he was sleeping peacefully. Blinking herself awake, she realized the noise was coming from the front doors of the clinic.

She stepped into the darkened hallway and closed Tyler's door behind her, not wanting anything to disturb the child. She could see two people outside in the covered entryway to the clinic, apparently having an argument.

Knowing she wasn't very visible with most of the clinic lights extinguished, she stepped close to the plate glass doors and looked out.

One of the people was Mary Lansing. The other, a man, Julia could only assume was her husband Lenny. And Lenny was in the process of hitting Mary.

Without thought, Julia unbolted the doors and yanked them open. "Stop it! Stop hitting her!"

The man turned on her as Mary tottered back, sobbing. He was wild-eyed, frenzied, with an insane, paranoid look on his face.

Too late, Julia recognized the signs of methamphetamine overdose. She's seen it often enough during her ER rotation in Portland. The patients were usually wild and out of control...and she was alone in the clinic with a sick child and a woman outside in the process of being beaten.

Julia turned and fled inside, forgetting to lock the door behind her. She made a grab for the phone at the receptionist's counter and dialed 911. When a calm woman answered, "911—what is your emergency?" she barked, "This is Dr. Julia Chambers at the Jasper Medical Clinic. I have some crazy guy outside high on methamphetamine who is beating up a woman—aaah!"

She gave a small scream. The phone dropped from her hand and clattered to the floor as Lenny Lansing barreled into her and actually lifted her high over his head before throwing her clear over the receptionist's counter. Julia crashed into the metal file cabinets and bounced onto the floor. She lay still, stunned. Her one rational thought was a concern for little Tyler, and she thanked God she'd closed the door to the room in which he was staying.

Lenny gave a roar but didn't come after her. Instead, it sounded like he was crashing around the waiting room, throwing chairs. Julia crawled back to the phone and picked it up. The line was dead, so she hoped the 911 operator had gotten the message and sent the police. Julia dialed Ben's phone number.

The phone rang and rang until the answering machine came on, while Julia crouched behind the counter and flinched every time she heard a crash. From the other end of the clinic, she heard Tyler start to cry, and then launch into a horrible coughing fit.

"C'mon, Ben, where are you?" she gritted. She heard a soft thud. She heard Mary Lansing give a queer gurgling scream. In frustration she slammed the phone down...then lifted her head as she heard another type of noise.

Curses. Threats. Men shouting. Julia lifted her

head over the counter, wincing at some new pain from being thrown, and looked into the waiting room.

Ben was there. He had cornered Lenny and tried to reason with him, but Julia knew from experience you couldn't reason with someone high on meth. Lenny swung a punch and Ben ducked, then plowed a fist into Lenny's jaw. Lenny staggered but fought back. Julia knew that meth users often had extraordinary strength in their strung-out bodies. Lenny wasn't about to be subdued.

She saw flashing lights and a sheriff's car screech into the parking lot. Two officers jumped out and ran into the clinic just as Lenny roared a threat and barged past Ben, punching him in the gut before charging the officers. They swung him around and struggled to put on handcuffs. Ben rose from his agonized bent-over position to help. Julia saw Mary Lansing sobbing on the floor just inside the door of the clinic, blood all over her face.

The noise was incredible as Lenny, foaming at the mouth, screamed and cursed and thrashed. Julia staggered to her feet and made her way down the hall to Tyler's room. The boy was bent double coughing and gagging, and even in the dim light of the nightlight she could see that his lips were blue.

Unfortunately there was nothing she could do. She could hold and comfort Tyler until his coughing eased, but she couldn't make him stop coughing. She could dart into the fray with Lenny Lansing, but she would only get hurt worse. Julia closed her eyes and gritted her teeth as the noise in the waiting room continued.

Finally the shouting eased and the noise stopped. Julia raised her head and listened. She edged Tyler back into bed where he dropped back to sleep, exhausted. Then she darted into the hallway to see what was up.

Lenny was on his stomach on the floor, handcuffed behind his back. He looked half-unconscious. Saliva trickled from his mouth and his nose was bleeding. Ben was on the floor with his fingers to Lenny's carotid artery, feeling his pulse. Two sheriff's officers—Todd Kempke and another man Julia didn't recognize—stood over Lenny's body.

"Classic symptoms of meth overdose," Ben was saying to the officers.

"Is there anything you can do for him?" asked Todd.

"No. There's no antidote for an overdose. All we can do is monitor his heartrate and blood pressure. And body temperature—sometimes it rises so high that they can die of hyperthermia, but I'm not getting that from him. He looks like he'll be okay."

"Then we'll lock him up until he comes down from his high." Todd reached down and jerked Lenny to his feet, where he sagged, head lolling. "Stupid bastard." He looked over at the corner of the room. "Mary, you okay?"

"Y-yes." Julia saw that Mary was crouched on a chair, curled up tight, with blood all over her face.

"We'll have to book him on possession," the other officer told Mary. "Ben can help you get patched up."

"Or I can." Julia stepped into the room. All eyes turned on her, and Ben gasped. "What happened to you?"

"Why? What's wrong?" Julia pushed a strand of hair out of her eyes.

Ben limped over and took her by the upper arms, examining her face. "Did he hit you?" he demanded.

"Not really. He tackled me, but he didn't hit me."

"Oh God." Ben closed his eyes for a moment. "You're all bruised and bloody."

"I am?"

"Yes. Probably in some shock too. Damn Lenny to hell." Ben released her arms and turned back to the officers. "Take him away before I strangle him."

"Mary." Julia went over and crouched next to the trembling woman. "Come on, Mary. Let's take a look at you." She lifted and half-supported the older woman to one of the exam rooms, flipping on the overhead light as she did so.

Mary's nose was swollen and obviously broken, and she had a nasty bruise on her right cheekbone, visible even under the blood. "We'll clean you up, Mary, and then inject a local anesthetic into your mouth. That will numb you up while we set your broken nose."

Ben came into the room with an ice pack. Together they worked on Mary, giving her ibuprofen and treating her nose. When the local took effect, they laid her on the exam table and inserted probes into her nasal passages to reset the bone. Then they packed her with gauze.

"Well, you're a pretty sight," said Julia lightly, as the helped her back into a sitting position.

"Thanks," said Mary in a muffled tone. She kept her eyes averted.

"Your turn," said Ben.

"Am I really that bad?"

"Yes," whispered Mary.

Julia walked over to the small mirror over the sink and gasped. "Oh wow. I had no idea."

She had scrapes and cuts all over her face. The shoulder of her shirt was torn, the side of her neck was scraped as if she'd run over gravel.

"Sit down," instructed Ben. "Mary, why don't you come with me? I'll have you just rest for a few minutes in another room."

After Ben walked out with Mary, Julia sat where he'd put her. The longer she sat, the worse she felt—bruised and battered and achy.

Ben came back in and knelt in front of her. "What did he do to you?" he asked. Was it her imagination, or did his voice tremble?

Julia closed her eyes for a moment. "I was so stupid," she mumbled. "I was dozing in Tyler's room when a noise woke me up. It was Lenny up front, hitting Mary. I didn't know who it was, of course—I just unlocked the door and went barging out. The moment he turned on me, I knew he was strung out on meth, so I ran inside and dove for the phone to call 911. He charged after me and literally picked me up. Tossed me right over the counter into Lisa's reception area. I crashed into the file cabinets. That's all, Ben—he hurt Mary a lot worse than he hurt me."

"I'm gonna press charges for assault," muttered Ben. "Attacking you that way."

"I'm fine, really I am."

"Tell me that in the morning, after you've slept. You'll wake up bruised and sore."

"So what are you doing here?" Julia glanced at the clock. "It's only 2:30, you said you wouldn't be here until three."

"Mary called me. She didn't know you were at the clinic, since it's usually closed at night. She called and said Lenny was sick, and she was bringing him into the clinic, and asked if I could meet her here." Ben's face was set in grim lines as he gathered gauze and ointment. "I had no idea the jerk was strung out on meth and would beat the holy crap out of you."

"*And* Mary."

"Yes. *And* Mary. But I don't have the urge to kill him over what he did to Mary. But if he showed up right now, I'd break his neck."

Warmth stole through her at his concern. "I'm fine, Ben. Really."

"Sure you are." Ben took some gauze smeared

with antibiotic cream and started to clean her cuts.

Julia bit her lip as pain ricocheted all over her while Ben attended to her wounds. In the aftermath of the crisis, she started to tremble.

"You okay?" asked Ben, pausing in his ministrations.

"Yes. Just delayed adrenaline." She closed her eyes, reliving the fear she'd felt when Lenny had thrown her bodily over the counter. "I'm just realizing that I could have broken a bone or two when Lenny threw me. I hit those file cabinets pretty hard."

Ben's jaw clenched. He dropped the tube of cream and yanked her against his chest. For a few precious moments, Julia allowed her vulnerability to surface. She leaned into Ben and took comfort from the strength of his arms around her, the heartbeat against her ear. What a wonderful man.

But wonderful men didn't last. She knew that all too well.

****

As Ben predicted, Julia woke the next morning stiff and sore and wretched. It was long past time when she normally went to work, but Ben had insisted she sleep in. She shuffled through her morning routine, swallowed some acetaminophen, and went to the clinic.

Lisa and Adele were putting things in order in the waiting room and reception area. "Man, Julia, you look terrible. How are you feeling?" asked Lisa, pausing as she scooped various items off the floor.

"Pretty sore," she admitted. She touched a bruised cheekbone. "But otherwise okay. It sure could have been worse."

"Never a dull moment around here, right?" said Adele. Both women looked at her with worried expressions on their faces.

"How's Tyler?"

"Home. Ben called the Doyles this morning and gave them strict instructions on how to care for him through the worst of the whooping cough." Adele smiled. "And—good news—they're going to vaccinate their children for polio."

"Hey, great!" Genuine relief went through Julia. "I'm happy to hear it!"

She went down the hallway to Ben's office. Gypsy, as usual, was curled up in her spot, though this time the dog launched herself at Julia the moment she walked in the door. "Hey, take it easy girl...okay, how's that?" She scratched the animal's neck while Ben watched her from behind his desk.

"How are you feeling?" he asked.

"Sore, just like you predicted. You look pretty washed out yourself." Ben had dark circles under his eyes.

"Quite the exciting night. Julia—are you up for a trip to Moscow today?"

"Sure, but why?"

"Mary Lansing has agreed to go to a battered women's shelter until she can make arrangements to move close to one of her children."

"Oh, Ben." Julia sat down heavily in one of the desk chairs. A smile lit her face. "That's the best news I've heard in a long time!"

"I thought you'd be pleased. But she wants you to take her, no one else."

"No problem."

"Why don't you just take the day off? You had a nasty scare last night—you're entitled. Take Mary in, and if you like you can toodle around Moscow all day, or whatever."

A softness—unwanted, and un-looked-for—filled Julia. "Thanks, Ben. Maybe I'll do that." She felt the familiar struggle inside her...the struggle against kindness. The feeling that any compassion that came her way should be resisted, because it wouldn't last.

Julia left the clinic and drove to Mary Lansing's older mobile home. Mary met Julia outside with two suitcases already packed. Her face was ugly and swollen, with bandages over her nose, bruises on her cheek, and dark circles under her eyes.

Julia hugged her, then held her at arms' length. "I'm glad you're going to the shelter, Mary. What changed your mind?"

"You should look in the mirror, Dr. Chambers." Mary's eyes filled with tears. "You have cuts all over your face. I felt so awful that Lenny hurt you. More than anything else, that's what convinced me. He needs help, and until he can get it, I guess I'd better not be around him."

"Smart woman. C'mon, let's get you into Moscow. I called the shelter in advance, and they know you're coming. They'll even have a private room for you, they said."

By the time Julia had settled Mary into the shelter, it was early afternoon. She stopped for lunch at the same Chinese restaurant she and Sandra had eaten in, then took Ben's advice and relaxed. She walked through the charming older sections of town, enjoying the store fronts and buildings.

She stopped for chai tea at a literary-looking coffee house full of an eclectic mix of earnest students and farmers in overalls. Books lined the dark-paneled walls, and the atmosphere was wonderfully...well, coffee-house-ish. Julia was charmed at once and decided to make this a regular stop whenever she was in Moscow.

Behind the coffee house was a used bookstore. Julia browsed the shelves until a title stopped her.

It was an older, battered, oversized book featuring popular landscape artists in the 1940's and 50's. What stopped Julia was that the painting featured on the front cover was the same as one of the rural prints on Ben's office wall.

She flipped through the book. It featured such artists as Walter Brightwell, Russell Moreton, and Robert Wood. All artists with which Ben was familiar. All landscapes of which he was fond. Julia held the book and thought carefully...

Ben would love this book, she knew. Yet the mere act of purchasing such a gift denoted a deeper intimacy, bonding, a deeper...well, commitment. And the familiar resistance surged up in her again.

Slowly she re-shelved the book and turned away. She couldn't do it. She couldn't.

She left the bookstore and continued strolling along the main street of the town. The trees were in summer bloom, vibrant and alive. The late afternoon sunshine was gentle. The people she passed were smiling. And she thought about that book.

A quick glance at her watch confirmed that the bookstore closed in five minutes. She hesitated, did an about-face, and hurried back to the store.

Sure enough, she pushed open the creaking door just as the proprietor was about to lock it. "I'm sorry, but do I have time to buy a book? I saw it earlier and I've been thinking about it."

"Sure," said the man. He stood aside and let her enter.

Julia dashed for the shelf, withdrew the book, and paid for it. As she left the bookstore with the volume clasped against her chest, she was amazed by the feeling of lightheartedness that accompanied her.

She drove back to Jasper in the early evening sunshine. The days were lengthening and she drove with her windows open, enjoying the sweet fresh air.

How to present him with the book? And when?

In the end, she let herself into the closed clinic and placed the book on his desk. He would find it the next day. She glanced at the four large rural prints on his walls and smiled. Yes, he would love the book.

146

She started to walk out of the office, then paused. The book. If it was a gift, then she should inscribe it. But what to say?

Slowly she went back to his desk and opened the book. On the inside front cover, she wrote, "To Ben, for showing me beauty. Julia."

The pictures in the book were beautiful...but nowhere near as beautiful as the things he had showed her in this obscure corner of Idaho.

She went home. It was nearly dark by now. As she went inside, the cat yowled and wound around her ankles with greater urgency than usual. With remorse, Julia realized she'd forgotten to fill his food bowl that morning.

"Oh cat, I'm sorry." Julia lifted down the bag of cat food and filled his bowl. Then she sat on a chair and watched him eat. When he'd gorged, he came and jumped on her lap, purring and rubbing his head affectionately against her hand.

"You're a forgiving soul," she told him. For some reason she blinked away tears. "Here I go and neglect you, yet you still love me. You stick around even though I ignore you at times. Why is that?"

In answer, he curled himself up on her lap, purring, and prepared to sleep. Julia leaned back against the chair and sighed as she scratched his neck. "I should give you a name," she told him. "I've had you now for over two months, you haven't left me yet, and here I'm still calling you 'cat.' What should I call you, I wonder?"

She looked at him carefully. He had two colors, orange and white. His tail was striped. Much of his underside was white except for an orange bib.

"With that bib, you look like a robin," she murmured. "Robin. That's a good name. Would you like being called Robin?"

The cat dug his neck into her fingers again, looking for affection.

147

"Maybe I should take you back to Portland with me," she murmured.

How long she sat in the darkening house, listening to the song of a late-singing meadowlark coming through the open window and smelling the sweet late spring/early summer air, she didn't know. But she was nearly dozing when the phone rang, jerking her upright and sending Robin fleeing from her lap.

She groped for the phone. "Hello?"

"It's Ben. I thought we'd have a quiet time of it after last night, but it seems I was wrong."

Tension clamped her stomach. "What's up?"

"It's Sara Johansen. She fell down the porch stairs. Meet me at the clinic."

Chapter Nine

It was no longer tension gnawing at the pit of her stomach as she raced the three blocks to the clinic—it was fear. Stark, raw fear.

No one was at the clinic yet, but Julia knew that wouldn't last. She prepared the anesthetic machine with fluoromethyl in case Sara required emergency surgery. She pulled out every medicine she could think of that she might possibly need. A rattling, annoying voice in the back of her mind kept up a stream of wishful thinking. *Maybe she's just bruised, but is otherwise fine. Maybe we'll take her to Gritman Medical Center in Moscow and they'll take care of her. Maybe this is just a scare and she'll be fine enough to go right back home again.* Maybe...just ...maybe...

Along with the panicky voice was another voice muttering medical information: horizontal versus vertical incisions, Friedman's curve, fetal distress procedures...

She heard a car drive up, and yanked a gurney through the front door of the clinic. Ben's car pulled into the parking lot at the same time. Julia pulled the gurney up to the passenger seat of the older Ford Escort while a man—presumably Gus Johanson, Sara's husband—dashed around the car.

"She's not too good," he gasped. "Took a bad fall down the stairs." His face was pale with fear.

Inside the car, Sara sat moaning with her hands wrapped around her large belly. She looked like any doctor's worst nightmare. Julia's heart was pounding so hard she wondered why she didn't faint at Sara's feet.

Instead she bent down. "Come on, Sara, let's get you up on the gurney," she said. With Ben's help, they got the woman onto the gurney, strapped her in, and rolled her into the clinic while Gus trotted alongside.

She knew damn good and well that Ben wasn't going to take charge of Sara. Yet. He'd told her he wouldn't hesitate to take over if she froze up, but Julia knew it was up to her to act like the professional she knew she was. She willed the fear away from her mind and replaced it with action.

"Ben, give Adele a call, ask her to come in. We'll need all the help we can get. Sara, let's get you here on the exam table—Gus, can you give me a hand?— that's it, Sara, good. On your left side, to take the pressure off the vena cava."

She yanked a blood pressure cuff over and wrapped it around Sara's arm. Her own heart was beating so loud that it was hard to hear Sara's readings, but she didn't like the result: 150/100.

"Damn," she muttered.

"What's the matter?" asked Gus.

"You're going to be a father before tonight is out," she said. "Gus, can I ask that you go into the waiting room? It won't be easy, I know, but we need to have you out of the way."

He nodded, smoothed back a strand from Sara's face, and leaned down to drop a kiss on her forehead. "I love you," he murmured.

With her eyes closed, Sara nodded. "Love you too," she whispered.

Conviction flowed into Julia. She wouldn't—she couldn't—let this couple down.

Ben came back into the room and automatically began scrubbing while Julia hooked up a fetal heart monitor. "Adele's on her way. What's the situation?"

"BP 160/110, heart rate 126," said Julia. "Looks like the fetus is suffering some distress, too—heart rate's 120 and dropping." She looked up at Ben. "We've got to get this baby out."

He nodded. "You go scrub. I'll bring her into the OR. As soon as Adele gets here, I'll have her call Moscow and arrange for a LifeFlight into Gritman."

"Just like Sandra," moaned Sara.

"We've got you covered, Sara," said Julia soothingly. She smoothed back a strand of the woman's hair. "How'd you like to hold your baby by the end of the night?"

A faint smile dusted Sara's face until a seizure abruptly took her.

"Damn," said Julia. "It's starting all ready." She whirled around, snatched up the syringe of magnesium sulfate she had prepared, and injected it intravenously. Within moments Sara's seizure stopped and Ben whisked the gurney into the clinic's small OR while Julia yanked surgical robes out of the cabinet and prepared to scrub.

Adele burst in. "What can I do?"

"Call Moscow and have them send a LifeFlight, and prepare a room for Sara and the baby. The baby's in distress so they'll need to alert the NICU. Then get into the OR and take over the fetal monitor."

Adele nodded and disappeared. Julia went into the OR and looked at Sara. Her eyes were rolling back, and her facial and hand muscles were twitching. For a moment, cold fear clutched her. This was all so familiar!

"She's going eclamptic!" she barked. Even as she spoke, Sara went into the tonic stage of eclampsia, where the twitching turned to clenching. Her arms and legs went rigid. Julia knew that that she had moments to hook Sara up to oxygen in case her respiratory muscles spasmed and caused her breathing to stop.

Julia's heart was pounding. In eclampsia, after the tonic stage came the clonic stage, where the patient frothed bloody saliva and the muscles jerked violently. Then came a coma or—sometimes—heart failure and death.

That's how she lost that patient in Portland. Julia clenched her teeth. She was *damned* if she'd let that happen again.

She began hooking Sara up to the anesthetic machine. The woman's eyes closed as the mask went over her face.

"You up to this?" asked Ben.

"Shut up," snapped Julia. "I'm scared to death. Don't distract me right now."

Ben grinned. "You're up to this, all right."

Adele came back in, scrubbed and robed, and took over the fetal monitor. "Fetal heart rate's 115," she said.

"Dropping," said Julia. "Distressed. We need to get this baby out."

She scrubbed and robed with lightening speed while Ben shaved and disinfected Sara's abdomen and Adele prepared the surgery tools.

"Ben, I'm going to make a vertical incision," she said as she picked up a scalpel. "We have no time to mess around with a Pfannenstiehl cut."

"Go for it."

Julia was vaguely aware that Adele appeared surprised at their role reversals—Julia in charge, Ben taking orders. But she had no time to dwell on it.

She paused, scalpel in hand, over Sara's abdomen. She closed her eyes and said a prayer. Then she took a deep breath and began gently slicing the woman's skin.

She pushed the incision down to the fascia, which lay under the fatty layer and over the abdominal muscles. She used scissors to cut the fascia horizontally toward each side, then pushed apart the two abdominal muscles to expose the peritoneum.

Using another pair of sharper, thinner scissors, Julia opened the peritoneum. She could see the bowel underneath the thin layer of tissue, and knew that if she nicked the bowel, Sara would have enormous complications. By the time the peritoneum was open, Julia was sweating profusely. Without a word, Adele reached over and mopped her forehead lest any sweat get in her eyes.

"Thanks," she muttered.

She enlarged the incision in the peritoneum, being careful not to cut too far down or she could damage Sara's bladder. She used a retractor to pull the lower part of the opening downward. Ben clamped it into place.

So far so good.

"Fetal rate 105," said Adele into the tense silence.

The retroperitoneal was visible now, lying just over the bulging uterus. "Hematoma," noted Julia. "Probably from where she fell down the steps."

"Where?" asked Ben.

"On the retroperitoneum."

"How bad?"

"Bad enough to cause her to go into premature labor." Julia made a small cut and incised vertically and pushed the bladder away where it rode up onto the lower part of the uterus. The movement made the retroperitoneum begin to bleed. But now she could see the uterus, bulging with the unborn baby. She could even see tiny movements within the womb.

She sponged up the blood then incised the uterus vertically, knowing as she did so that she was dooming Sara to C-sections for any future children she had. But it was better than losing the baby in there right now.

"Ben, the moment I get the baby out, leave Sara to me. You and Adele will have to make sure he can breathe on his own. Got the laryngoscope?"

"Right here," said Adele. "The bulb aspirator, too."

"Okay, here goes." Julia lifted the baby from Sara's womb while Ben sucked out the amniotic fluid. "It's a girl." She handed the baby to Ben while Adele leaned over and aspirated the infant's nose and mouth. Meanwhile, Julia clamped and cut the umbilical cord. "Now get going."

Ben laid the baby on the warming table while Julia turned back to Sara. She knew that Ben would first insert the laryngoscope down the baby's throat to locate the trachea, then insert the tube while Adele hooked it up to an anesthetic bag attached to the oxygen machine.

Meanwhile, she separated the placenta from the uterine wall and laid it aside, noting that she hadn't heard the baby cry yet. Bad sign. But she had to sew Sara up first before she could turn any attention to the infant. Julia knew the baby was in good hands at the moment. Besides, Sara was bleeding heavily from the hematoma, and needed her attention.

She checked the uterus to make sure no part of the placenta was left over. Frowning, she noticed some of the tissue still adhering to the uterine wall. She scraped it off. Sara was still bleeding, but Julia didn't think it was enough to signify postpartum hemorrhaging. Julia put oxytocin into Sara by her IV in order to speed contraction of the uterus. Then she tilted the uterus through the incisions and began sewing Sara up with dissolvable stitches.

"She's going pink," said Ben from behind her. "Let's take out the tube and see if she'll breathe on her own."

154

A good sign.

Julia slipped the uterus back into Sara's pelvis and started suturing the bladder flap. From behind her she heard Ben say, "She's paling. Let's reinsert."

Julia whipped around. "The baby's not breathing yet?"

"Not yet." Ben's mouth was set as he reinserted the tube down the tiny trachea. "We're working on her."

A bad sign.

Julia turned back to Sara, heart beating fast but knowing she had to concentrate on the task at hand. She left the peritoneum alone, knowing that to suture it was unnecessary and might cause adhesions later on. Instead she loosely tied together the abdominal muscles in three spots to keep them in place.

She concentrated on repairing the fascia, using thicker and more durable sutures. Since the fascia is the main support layer of the abdomen, it was critical to repair it correctly.

"That baby breathing yet?" she asked.

"Not yet. Adele, let's remove the tube and see how she does."

Julia sutured the skin of the abdomen just below the surface. She turned to the warming table where Ben and Adele hovered over the infant, who looked too pale and bluish.

"Back in," snapped Ben. He reinserted the tube and began pumping oxygen, while bent over the tiny chest with his stethoscope, listening to the heartbeat.

Suddenly the baby's arms and legs began to move feebly, and she looked like she was fighting the tube in her throat. Ben pulled the tube out, and the baby took two quick breaths and let out a squall. Relief flooded Julia, and she exchanged grins with Ben and Adele under their masks.

"That's my girl," murmured Adele in a thick, teary voice.

"She's hemorrhaging," said Ben suddenly.

Julia jerked around and saw that Sara had enormous amounts of blood flowing from her vagina. "More pitocin," snapped Julia. Ben leaped over to increase the flow of oxytocin in the IV. All Julia could do was catch the blood in a basin as it poured out of Sara's body. Sara was bleeding so heavily that Julia knew she could lose four pints within minutes...and the clinic didn't have the ability to do a blood transfusion. If Sara lost too much blood, she would go into hypovolemic shock and die.

"Is her uterus atonic?" asked Ben.

Julia palpated the uterine fundus. "No, it's that hematoma. Ben, increase the oxytocin to twenty units. Dammit Sara, stop bleeding." Blood flowed down Julia's wrists as she withdrew her hand from the woman's uterus. Julia was sweating again, praying the pitocin would work.

The tense seconds ticked by until abruptly, the bleeding lessened and then reduced to a trickle...and Julia knew the crisis was over.

As she started to clean Sara up, her hands trembled. She knew she had come within a hair's breath of losing another patient. Post-partum hemorrhaging was one of the most uncontrollable and frightening complications from childbirth. Even if the clinic had blood available, they couldn't replace it in Sara's body faster than it was being lost.

She blinked back tears and heard helicopter blades chopping overhead as LifeFlight approached and prepared to land in the clinic parking lot.

"Give her 250 micrograms of ergonovine IM," she told Ben. "That's the best we can do under these conditions to keep her stable until she gets to the ICU in Moscow."

"We should go talk to Gus. He's probably scared

to death."

"I'll talk to him." Julia pulled off her sterile gloves and went to prepare the new father for his wife's condition.

****

Ben saw Gus, Sara, and their new daughter into the medical helicopter for the flight into Moscow. Then he went back into the clinic.

Adele was cleaning up the operating room, but Julia was not with her, as he expected. Nor was she in the receptionist's area or the exam room. He went down the hall and poked his head into her office. Empty.

Puzzled, he nosed into his own office…and found her sprawled on one of his cracked leather office chairs, illuminated by a single desk lamp. Her head was back, her eyes were closed, her mouth had lines of suffering around it.

"Julia?"

No answer. Incredibly, it seemed she had dropped off to sleep.

Ben felt a welling up of love as he never had before, watching her quiet breathing. She had faced her fears and conquered them. She had won the battle.

God, she was beautiful. He watched the shine of her dark hair in the lamplight. She had a flush on her cheeks and huge bloodstains on her scrubs. A red line on her forehead and cheeks indicated where the surgical mask had lain. To Ben, she was the epitome of everything he had ever looked for in a woman.

He slipped around the desk and sat in his own chair, feeling privileged just to watch her. Smack in the middle of his desk was a book…a large, older book of art.

He leafed through it and saw many of his favorite artists dating back five or six decades. He glanced at one of the prints on his wall by Walter Brightwell, and saw a biography of the artist in the book, along with a number of pictures of the artist's works.

What a wonderful book—but where did it come from? He glanced at Julia—had she brought it for him? If so, when?

He noticed some writing on the inside front cover and paused to read it: "To Ben, for showing me beauty. Julia."

Beauty. What kind of beauty? The beauty of Jasper in the summer? The beauty of an intimate relationship? The beauty—he glanced at her—of conquering her professional fears?

Whatever her meaning, it was a treasured inscription.

In a few minutes, Julia's hand slipped off her lap and jerked her awake. She lifted her head and rubbed her eyes, while Ben watched her come awake.

"Good morning," he said.

"Hmmmm. Sorry, must have dropped off. Sara?"

"On her way to Gritman." Ben closed the book and folded his hands upon it. "Do you want your procedural review now or later?"

He saw wariness spring to her eyes. "Now. Get it over with."

"That was, without doubt, one of the finest handlings of an emergency case I've ever seen. You really did your homework, Julia."

Julia laid her head back and stared at the ceiling. "Thank God," she whispered. He saw a tear slide down one cheek.

"Hey—hey—what's wrong?"

More tears trickled down. She sniffed and raised her head. "I was so scared, Ben. I was scared spitless that I was going to lose her. Or the baby."

"Every doctor has those moments. The

158

important thing is that you didn't panic. You didn't even freeze up." He let out a breath. "And there's no doubt that those types of cases are *not* what this clinic is designed to handle."

"These types of cases are also what *general practitioners* are not designed to handle."

"Amen. It made me realize, though, that we need blood here." He drew a shaky breath. "We almost lost her. If that post-partum hemorrhaging had continued, she would have gone into shock, and there wouldn't have been a damn thing we could have done about it."

"I know."

"You did well, Julia. Sara's situation was so much more complex than Sandra's. Sandra didn't have PPH, or a hematoma emergency to deal with, or a baby in distress. Yet you handled everything beautifully. Dr. Schweitzer will be pleased."

Startled, she stared at him. "What does Dr. Schweitzer have to do with this?"

"He called here a couple of weeks ago, asking about your progress and seeking a performance review."

Her cheeks flushed. "You never told me that!"

"No, sorry, somehow I never got around to it. I told him to truth about your performance here—how you blundered it with Sandra, but how well you handled Jake Smothers."

"You told him about Sandra?" The flush in her cheeks paled.

"Yes. Of course. I also told him how I put you in charge of Sara, and how hard you'd been studying up on all the possibilities in her case. I told Schweitzer that it was an opportunity to redeem yourself, and he agreed. He's going to be very pleased with your conduct of this evening."

He watched her lips compress. "I don't know whether to be furious or pleased."

"Why should you be furious?"

"To not mention to me that you were talking to Dr. Schweitzer behind my back..."

"Julia, in case you've forgotten, I'm your boss." Ben folded his hands on top of the book and kept his expression neutral. "Unless or until you come to us as a full-fledged doctor and a partner at this clinic, it's my responsibility to report your performance to your precept. I was not talking to Dr. Schweitzer behind your back. He called me, and I gave him a performance review. Nothing ominous about it."

She dropped her eyes and didn't say anything.

Ben picked up the book. "Is this yours?"

She nodded but didn't smile. "No, it's yours. I saw it in Moscow this afternoon, when I was browsing around after I settled Mary into the shelter. I...well, I thought of you right away when I saw it."

"It's great." He flipped through the pages again, touched. "I'm a sucker for those types of paintings, so I couldn't ask for a better gift." He closed the book again. "But why did you buy it?"

"Why not?"

He was quiet a moment. "Call me foolish, but somehow I'm reading more into this than just a gift between friends. The inscription you wrote says that. Or am I wrong?"

"No." She shifted in her chair. "You're not wrong. I suppose I wanted to give you something to remember me by. I—I'm leaving shortly, Ben. My rotation here is up in two weeks."

He felt anger flash through him, but he masked it and kept his voice even. "You don't *have* to leave, you know."

"Yes I do. I have one more rotation to complete before I finish my residency. Dr. Schweitzer feels it would be useful to do this rotation in internal medicine."

"You're a senior resident, Julia. You have a lot of say in where you go next to complete your residency requirements. Don't you feel as if you've gotten some excellent training here?"

"Yes, but Dr. Schweitzer said..."

"Dr. Schweitzer said it's up to *you* to make that decision. I mentioned to Schweitzer about the possibility of you staying on here, and completing your rotation. He agreed that your training has been outstanding, and endorsed that option. So it's up to you now. You can go back to Portland if you want, or you can stay here and continue doing miracles."

She jerked her head up. "I'm not doing miracles, I'm doing my job."

"Explain that to Mabel Smothers. Or Sara Johanson."

"And why can't I do miracles just as well in Portland as here?"

"Because in Portland, there are lots of doctors. We don't have that luxury here. Besides, Julia..." He leaned forward. "Have you thought about what you'll do after you complete your residency? You're a GP. You can work within the hospital system, of course, but then you'd never get to know your patients personally. Or you can set up your own office, but I'm sure you're aware of just how much that would cost. Or you can go to work at an office that's already set up, and be the lowest person on the totem pole. Or....you can stay here. You've already made an excellent impression with the local population. It's a hell of a good way to start a career."

"I—I can't stay here."

Anger flashed in him again. "Why not?"

He saw her pause, as if struggling with something. "I just can't."

"That's hardly a reason. We've been through a lot in the last few months. Is nothing we've shared worth a damn to you?"

161

"It *is* worth a damn. It's just that..."

"It's just that you're running scared again."

"Ben—"

"What's putting you off, Julia? Is it the size of Jasper?"

"No..."

"The local people? The limitations of our medical facility?"

"No..."

"Is it *me?*"

She bit her lip and said nothing.

"I see," said Ben. "So falling in love with you was obviously the wrong thing for me to do."

She stared at him with a stunned look on her face. "In *love* with me?"

"Julia. Hasn't it been obvious? I fell in love with you weeks ago. What did you think—that I was just having sex with you for mere lust?" He lowered his voice. "I can't imagine a more perfect woman for me. You're everything I've ever dreamed of. What more can I tell you?"

"You...you *can't* be in love with me." Her voice was flat. Cold.

Whatever reaction Ben had expected, it wasn't this. She acted as if being in love with her was something dreadful.

Tucked into his desk drawer was a small box containing a diamond ring that he'd bought the last time he was in Moscow. Ben had a sudden, alarming vision that it might just stay there.

So, being careful, he kept his voice neutral. "So this emotion is not reciprocated?"

"No!" Her answer was too fast, almost panicky. "No, it's not!"

"I see. Then what we've shared *isn't* worth a damn to you."

"Don't start, Ben." She scrubbed a hand over her face. "I couldn't handle it tonight."

"Then go home, Julia." He rose from his chair. He left the book on the desk. "Go home before I say something I might regret later. But think carefully." He leaned forward to emphasize his words. "In the middle of the night, when you wake up by yourself, think carefully about whether all the running away is getting you anyplace." He straightened up. "Lock up as you leave. Goodnight, Julia."

****

Julia sat in the chair in Ben's office for a few minutes after he'd left. She felt exhausted, but this time not from the surgery. Instead, she felt beaten down from Ben's arguments.

Stay here. Return to Portland. Stay here. Return to Portland.

She buried her face in her hands. Oh God, she wanted to stay here. And Ben said he was in love with her. But she knew better. Ben wouldn't last. No one in her life lasted. His love would dry up, and she would be alone once more.

And so she would leave. She would leave to protect herself. *A rock feels no pain. An island never cries.* She would be a rock and an island if it killed her.

She rose from the chair, feeling very old. She began stripping off her surgical scrubs as she made her way to the operating room, where Adele was just finishing up the cleaning.

"That was a good job you did, Julia," said Adele, wiping down surfaces with antibacterial solution.

"Thanks." Julia crumpled the surgical robe into a bundle. "Man I'm tired, though. I sure hope Sara and the baby will be okay."

"Gritman has an excellent NICU," Adele replied. "The baby will be fine, especially since she was breathing on her own. As for Sara—well, if she doesn't develop HELPP syndrome, she'll be right as rain inside a couple of weeks."

"Need help here?"

"No, I'm almost done. Go home and get some sleep."

"I think I will. Thanks for being Johnny-on-the-spot tonight, Adele."

"Hey, it's my job." Adele smiled. "And I have to admit, there's something to being in a place where I know all the patients. It will be fun to watch Sandra and Sara raise their kids."

"Yeah. Fun. G'night, Adele."

Julia drove home and parked her car in the driveway. She sat for a moment in the silent car, listening to the sound of the crickets and the faint hoot of a great horned owl coming from the woods that surrounded Jasper. Then she went inside to greet Robin, who meowed and curled around her ankles with affection.

Julia sat down on the sofa, hauled the cat onto her lap, and burst into tears.

She'd never see Sandra or Sara again. She wouldn't be around to watch their babies grow up. She'd leave here, do her last rotation in Portland, and probably stay in that city—or some other city—for the rest of her life.

"Damn it all, why am I crying?" she asked Robin. "This should be my moment of triumph. I saved Sara's life."

She sobbed harder. Her moment of triumph had turned to ashes in light of Ben's pressure to stay here. In light of his declaration of love.

Why couldn't she accept it? Why couldn't she take the easy route—return his love, stay in Jasper, get married, have kids....

Because she couldn't. Life *wasn't* easy, and things didn't last. *Love* didn't last.

She was in a damning mood. She damned her father for walking out on her when she was a child. To grow up without a man in the house made her

164

wary of men's intentions.

She damned her mother for abandoning her as a teenager. What kind of mother could do that? How could a mother abandon her own child? Julia could only conclude during those hormone-laden impressionable years that her mother left because she, Julia, was unlovable.

And she damned Alex for confirming that conclusion. Except now, oddly, he seemed to want her back. Julia's natural caution made her wonder why.

And Ben...

Julia sobbed harder.

Ben, whose firm hand had guided her through her worst professional fears. Whose gentle hand had shown her the wonders of physical love. And whose constant, unrelenting pressure to stay was tying her up in knots. And whose unexpected statement of love made her go cold with dread.

How could she stay in Jasper and risk—eventually—having Ben leave her too? Far better to sever the relationship now, on her *own* terms, and keep her emotions intact. Far better to look upon Ben as a spring fling and leave it at that. Far better to be a rock and an island.

Dammit.

Chapter Ten

"I'll be leaving in a week," said Julia to Sandra Kempke.

"You can't go," said Sandra flatly. She lifted her infant son onto her shoulder. "I won't let you. Besides, if you leave next week, you won't be around when Sara and the baby are released from the hospital."

Julia smiled, though there was sadness on her face. "Part of me really wants to stay, but I have to return to Portland."

"Why do you *have* to return to Portland?"

"Well, I have one more rotation to complete before I'm considered a full-fledged doctor..."

"So, complete it here."

"I...I can't."

"It's Ben, isn't it?" asked Sandra, with the same deadly feminine precision Julia had noted earlier.

And for once, Julia decided to be honest. "Yes," she confessed. "Here, let me hold the baby for awhile." She took the tiny infant out of Sandra's arms, and gently laid him on her shoulder. "Yes, it's Ben," she admitted.

"So you're running *away* from him? You should be running *toward* him."

"You make it sound so simple."

"Well, isn't it? What's the deal, then?"

Julia was quiet a moment, softly rubbing little Aaron's back as she wondered how to answer. "I suppose it's because I can't believe he's for real," she said. "What I mean is, all my life the people I love eventually leave me." She gave Sandra an abbreviated sketch of her rocky childhood. "Then when Alex left me, I suppose it reinforced that there's something about me that people don't like, or that turns them off, or whatever. At any rate, if I let myself...well, fall in love with Ben, then deep down I know it's just a matter of time before he leaves, too. Then I'll hurt like crazy."

"Welcome to real life," observed Sandra. "You take chances. Now let's get down to brass tacks. Take this Alex, for example. What do you think *you* did that made him leave you? No, don't answer that right away," she added, when Julia opened her mouth to reply. "What I mean is, did Alex leave you because you suddenly became a nag that he couldn't stand to be around? Or did he leave you because he's a jerk and not worth the time of day?"

Julia wasn't about to mention her emotional aftermath of the patient who had died on her. However she saw where Sandra was heading. "I suppose he was a jerk," she admitted.

"There!" Sandra smiled. "Though why you would become engaged to a jerk is beyond me."

"Ben asked the same thing."

"Oh ho! So you two *have* discussed it."

"Of course. But it makes no difference. My judgment of men is obviously off."

"Not always. You couldn't do much better than Ben. He's type that sticks around for the long haul."

Julia shook her head and closed her eyes. The fear that welled up in her at the mere thought was staggering. "I can't," she mumbled. "I just can't." She felt the weight of little Aaron on her shoulder, and a part of her wondered if she would ever feel the weight of her *own* child on her shoulder.

"You're a fool, Julia," said Sandra quietly.

"Maybe so." Julia lifted Aaron down and handed him back to his mother. "But at least I'm a *safe* fool."

****

The office was quiet. Ben, who had been avoiding her for the last two weeks, was out on a call. Lisa and Adele had gone to lunch together to celebrate Lisa's birthday.

The phone rang. "Good afternoon, Jasper Medical Clinic," said Julia.

"I'd like to speak to Dr. Chambers," said a woman's wispy voice.

"This is Dr. Chambers," replied Julia. "Mrs. Lansing, is that you?"

"Yes. Dr. Chambers, I just wanted to call and say thank-you."

"How are you doing?"

"Much better. The nice folks here at the shelter have made me realize what I've been putting up with from Lenny for all this time. I—I see now that I can't help him myself, that he has to help himself first."

Julia was silent a moment, thinking about the testimony she had given Sheriff Todd Kempke last week about Lenny's assault. He was being booked on methamphetamine possession and manufacture, domestic violence, and assault. She had a feeling he was going to be in jail for quite some time.

"You're quite right, Mary," she said. "Any changes have to come from within your husband. How is your nose? And your fingers?"

"Both fine, thank you. Or rather, getting better. I just wanted to let you know that I'll be moving to Lewiston to be near one of my sons." Julia could hear a smile creep into the woman's voice. "He's been after me since he moved away from home, to come live near him. I'll try not to step on his toes too much, but I'm looking forward to moving."

"I'm so happy for you, Mary," said Julia. "This means a lot to me, that you'll be safe. You see, I'll be leaving here and going back to Portland next week

168

to finish my residency there. Knowing that you're okay means that you won't be haunting me in my sleep."

Mary Lansing gave a charming little chuckle, and Julia realized it was the first time she'd heard the woman laugh. "Best of luck to you then," she said.

Julia hung up the phone lighter of heart. *One loose end tied up*, she thought.

****

"I thought the polio vaccine was given on sugar cubes," said Retta Doyle, watching as Julia prepared a syringe to vaccinate two of her three children.

"Sometimes it is. However, the oral polio vaccine is a live vaccine. Something like one out of 2.5 million people who receive the OPV actually get polio." She could feel Retta tense up. "But the inactivated polio vaccine—which is what this is—is wonderful. It's never been known to cause serious problems, and about the worst thing that can happen—besides a sore spot from the needle, of course—is an allergic reaction. Yet even that possibility is small."

Mrs. Doyle bit her lip as Julia laid the two prepared syringes aside. "What are you waiting for?"

"I'm waiting to see if you have any other questions first. While I think you're doing the right thing, I don't want to just grab your kids and inject them if you still have concerns."

"How long before Tyler can get his shots?"

"We have to wait for him to recover completely from the whooping cough, so it'll be a few months. You've been very good about nursing him through, and the erythromycin spared the other kids from getting whooping cough as well."

Retta sighed. "Okay, go ahead and vaccinate John and Loretta."

Within minutes both children had received the

first of their shots. Julia placed a hand on Retta Doyle's shoulder. "Thank you," she said. "You've done the right thing."

Retta looked more at ease since her children were not keeling over on the spot. She even smiled at Julia as she shepherded her kids out of the clinic.

Another loose end tied up, thought Julia.

****

"You'll have scarring, but I just don't see any problems with regaining full use of your arm," said Julia. She rotated and flexed Jake Smothers' left forearm and put it through the full range of motion. "What kind of problems are you still having?"

"I can't grab things tightly yet," said Jake. When Julia released his arm, he flexed his wrist and rubbed the muscles, clearly from force of habit. "I'll try to pick something up, and if it's too heavy it crashes to the floor."

"And usually breaks," added Mabel with a smile. "Meaning *I'm* the one that has to clean it up."

"Who usually milks your cow?"

"I do," said Mabel.

"Jake, I'd like to have you take over the milking," said Julia. "I can't think of a better physical therapy for your arm and hand than squeezing an udder twice a day. Go easy at first—Mabel, you should stand by and be ready to take over when his arm tires—but Jake, that'll help heal you up faster than any fancy exercises I can give you."

She knew she'd scored another point with the Smothers when unwitting respect flared in Jake's eyes. "I'll do that, Dr. Chambers," said Jake. "It ain't gonna be a hardship to get better by making sure we get our milk every day."

Julia nodded and prepared to leave. "I should let you know that I won't be back," she said. "I'm returning to Portland in a few days to finish my residency there."

"Is that so!" exclaimed Mabel in dismay. She shook her head. "Imagine going to a place like Portland."

Julia couldn't help but chuckle. "It's not so bad," she said. "Though I've gotten to like Jasper a lot more than I thought I would."

"We'll be sorry to lose you, Dr. Chambers," said Jake gruffly. He held out his right hand. "Thank you for saving my arm."

Mabel followed her to the door. "I made some more cookies for you, Dr. Chambers," she said shyly, offering Julia a large box. "I can't tell you how grateful we are, you helpin' Jake like you did."

"Thank you, Mabel!" exclaimed Julia. The box must have weighted ten pounds. "I put those cookies you gave me last time in the clinic's lunch room, and they were gone in a week."

"Well, take these with you back to Portland," insisted Mabel. "It'll be a taste of home for you. You take of yourself, hear? And...and thanks once again."

Julia's eyes were stinging as she bounced down the rutted dirt road back toward Jasper. The box on the seat next to her bounced as well. Those cookies would, indeed, be a taste of home when she was back in Portland.

****

Julia watched the little girl skip over the gravel sidewalk towards a pickup truck. A necklace with a tube hanging from it bounced on her shirt front. There was something familiar about her, something that nagged at her mind...until she saw the shaggy man following behind, carrying sacks from the grocery store.

Of course. It was Clem Parker, and the girl was his daughter Jessie who had gone into anaphylactic shock after that bee sting in her neck.

Julia hurried over. "Mr. Parker!"

The man paused in the act of opening up the truck's door. He stared at her for a moment, not recognizing her. Then he smiled, a slow sweet smile. "Aren't you one of the doctors from the clinic?"

She held out her hand. "Julia Chambers, that's right."

Clem dropped his grocery bags on the ground and nearly pumped her arm from its socket. "How can I ever thank you enough for saving my girl?" he asked.

Julia turned to the bright-eyed child. "And how are you, Jessie?"

"Fine, thank you ma'am," said the child. Her diction was remarkably clear. "I'm six years old now."

"Are you! You're getting big. I helped you out when you got sick after that bee sting."

"Daddy said you saved my life," said the girl matter-of-factly. "Thank you."

Julia laughed. "You're a bright little thing," she said. "Your daddy's homeschooling you, isn't he?"

"Yes ma'am. I just started addition," she added proudly. "And in science, we're studying rocks. And I'm helping him write a book!"

Julia laughed again as she turned to Clem. "A little biased in the sciences, aren't we?"

"Welllll," he drawled, "maybe I am. I'm writing a children's book on geology now, and Jessie's helping."

Julia's eyes dropped to a bulge under Clem's shirt, one that matched the tube necklace hanging around Jessie's neck. "I see you're carrying an epinephrine kit."

Clem Parker touched the tube. "We don't go anywhere without our kits, do we Jessie?"

"Nope. Daddy says I should never take it off when I'm outside."

God, what a cute kid. Julia squatted down to

Jessie's level. "Your daddy's a smart guy," she told the girl. She ruffled the child's hair. "I'm glad you have each other."

"Daddy, daddy!" Jessie tugged on her father's sleeve as Julia straightened up. Clem bent down to hear his daughter's whispered question. He grinned and glanced at Julia. "She wants to know if you can come out to our place for dinner some time. I should warn you, she *loves* inviting people to dinner because she likes my cooking."

How could she ever have thought that Clem Parker was someone to run screaming from in a dark alley? She was touched, down to her toes. "Aw, Jessie—I'd love to, but I'm leaving town in a week."

"Leaving?" exclaimed Clem. "Where?"

"I have to return to Portland and finish my residency."

"Oh." Jessie cast her eyes downward.

Clem reached out to shake her hand once more. "I'm sorry to hear that," he said. "But I'll always remember what you did for Jessie. Thank you."

****

Julia went into Ben's office and closed the door behind her. Gypsy thumped her tail from the corner. Ben looked up from a file on his desk and said nothing as she seated herself in one of the cracked leather chairs.

"I'm ready to leave, Ben."

"I figured as much." He leaned back in his chair and waited.

This was almost the first time they'd spoken privately in over two weeks. Julia felt irrational annoyance at his stand-offish attitude, but she didn't voice it. She knew he was employing the precise same defense mechanism *she* was—separating himself from being too involved with her as she prepared to leave his life.

"You've been a fantastic teacher. Thank you,"

she said.

"You've been a fantastic resident. I appreciate you helping me through a rough patch."

Silence, pregnant with emotion, swirled around them. Julia felt the sting of tears in her eyes, and blinked them away. "Yes. Well. Good-bye, then."

"Julia, you're being an idiot," said Ben. For the first time, she noticed he was clenching his fists. "You're running back to Portland to work under a man who will squash you under this thumb."

"Alex won't squash me under his thumb," she countered. "I'm a strong person, Ben. I'm all grown up. I can stand on my own two feet."

"Those are great clichés, but the fact remains that the man dumped you when you needed him, at a time when you *weren't* all grown up. And now you're going to work for him?" He shook his head.

Julia spoke angrily because she knew Ben was right. "Look, just because *you're* insecure that I'll be working under my ex-fiancé..."

"Insecure?" Ben's eyes bugged out. "Dammit, Julia, *you're* the one who's insecure! It's not so much this Alex guy that worries me, it's *you!*" He pounded his desk. "Remember, Julia—*you're* the one running away. *I'm* the one staying right here. Think about it." He jerked his head toward the door. "Now get out of here before I say something I'll regret."

Julia fled.

****

She drove the nearly 500 mile trip from Jasper, Idaho to Portland, Oregon in nine hours.

For the first two hundred miles, she alternately cried and sniffed. For the rest of the trip she stared with stony silence at the gray highway in front of her.

She was a rock, after all. An island. She had no need of friendship—friendship caused pain. Just like the old song said.

In a cardboard carton on the seat beside her was the chink in her armor: Robin. He had meowed piteously for those first few terrible hours, but now he lay quiet.

"You're the first pet I've ever had," she told him at one point. "Promise you won't walk out on me?"

There was no answer, of course, but deep down Julia knew what Robin would reply if he could: Don't leave *me*, and I won't leave *you*.

Remember, Julia—you're the one running away. I'm the one staying right here. Think about it.

It wasn't too late. She could turn her car around and be back in Jasper before nightfall.

Five hours later she drove into Portland, unfortunately arriving just in time for rush hour traffic.

It took some getting used to. For three months she had lived in a place where she could cross the main street of the town without hardly looking. And now...

Now there were cars and trucks and busses and highways and construction and buildings and people everywhere. Julia loved Portland—she truly did—but at the moment it was a little hard to take.

By the time she drove up to the resident housing across the street from the Portland City Hospital, she was exhausted. She gathered up Robin in his box and found her room key. She was already in the building before she remembered to go back and lock her car.

In her dorm-like room, she opened the box and let Robin out. He lifted his and looked at his new surroundings with deep, feline suspicion. Julia suddenly remembered why she had never had a pet: a resident's hours were long and erratic, and now Robin would be always confined to these two small rooms for the indefinite future.

No mice for him to chase. No robins for him to

stalk. She couldn't just open the back door and let him outside while she was at work, to do what cats like to do.

"I'll buy you come cat toys first thing," she promised him. "At least that will give you something to do while I'm gone." She knew, however, that to a cat who was used to outside access, this was a poor substitute.

Julia sighed. "This is just the first of many trials to come," she muttered. For now that the time was at hand, she dreaded the idea of starting a rotation with her former fiancé.

However, at this stage she had little choice in the matter. Early on Monday morning, she walked across the street to the hospital and found Alex's office.

"Julia!" He rose from his desk and kissed her on the cheek. "It's good to see you. You're looking well."

"Hello, Alex." She refrained from returning any of his greetings. She didn't want to lie. It *wasn't* good to see him.

How could she ever have thought that Ben wasn't as handsome as Alex? Oh sure, Alex was well-groomed and model-sleek in his looks. But he lacked Ben's earthy charm, his open and frank expression.

Alex had Nordic good looks, with blond hair and blue eyes. Suddenly, though, he seemed artificial and affected.

Alex walked Julia through his department and outlined her hours and duties. There was nothing worrying about the day, but Julie was left with a queasy feeling inside her at the thought of being at Alex's beck and call for the next three months.

"Join me for lunch," said Alex, and they headed for the hospital's cafeteria. "And you can tell me about this little place where you spent the spring."

"It was quite nice, actually," said Julia.

Alex raised a single eyebrow. "It was?"

"Yes. I—"

"Julia!"

Julia turned and saw Pat Schweitzer heading towards her. He pumped her hand while she smiled. She'd always liked Pat.

"I heard you staged quite a remarkable emergency C-section and managed to save both the mother and the baby!" he remarked.

Obviously he'd been talking with Ben. Julia was filled with gratitude that he chose this moment to highlight her accomplishments, in Alex's hearing. "That's right," said Julia.

Alex lifted that damned eyebrow again. "You did?"

Suddenly Julia was pissed. She turned to Alex and snapped, "That's right, I did."

"Post-partum hemorrhaging, seizures, eclampsia, retroperitoneal hematoma," rumbled Pat, ticking off Sara Johanson's complications on his fingers. "You'll make a hell of a GP, Julia. One of our best, in fact."

Julia smiled sweetly. "Thanks, Pat." She was pleased to note Alex squirming beside her.

With sudden clarity, she realized what had always bugged her about Alex: he didn't believe she could succeed without his mentoring and support. The fact that Julia had not only conducted herself well in Jasper, but managed to overcome her worst professional fears—without Alex's help—probably bothered him no end.

Good.

****

The following Saturday, Julia did want she'd wanted to do for three months: she went to a Starbuck's café, ordered her favorite cappuccino, and sat back to absorb the atmosphere.

Ahhhh, this was better. This was what she'd

missed most about Portland—the cafés where one could sit and watch the world go by.

Of course—she looked at her cup—the coffee from Betty's Café in Jasper was just as good. Maybe even better. And while the atmosphere was nice, she recalled the literary coffee house in Moscow that was full on an eclectic mix of earnest students and farmers in overalls. What a fabulous place that had been.

Well, phooey. With a shock, Julia realized she was losing her taste for Portland. Not good.

****

"Here's the MRI on Janet Sloan," said Julia, handing Alex several printouts. "If you look here, and here, it confirms that she does have lung cancer. The blood tests show the same results."

"If the stupid bitch would stop smoking, this wouldn't be happening," said Alex.

Julia stiffened. "That's the irony of the whole thing," she replied. "If you remember, Janet Sloan *doesn't* smoke. However, she's at the N-zero stage, so her prognosis is good."

"Fine. Whatever. Listen, Julia—what do you say to dinner tonight?"

Startled at the change of subject, Julia looked at him. His blue eyes were dark with desire, a look she remembered all too well. He might be saying *dinner*, but what he meant was *sex*. "No, thank you," she replied.

He raised his eyebrow. "What kind of an answer is that?" he answered. "I made reservations at that Italian place you like so well. It'll be just like old times."

Julia slapped the file folder shut. "No, it *won't* be just like old times," she snapped. "We're not an item any more, Alex, thanks to your treatment of me after I lost that patient. And if you keep up with these proposals, I can only assume you wanted me to do

178

my last residency with you solely in order to get me back in your bed."

"So what's wrong with that?" Alex scowled. "We were good together, Julia."

"We might have been good in bed, but that's about it. If you love someone, you're supposed to support them during the bad times. You dumped me instead."

"Look, if you're going to hold that one incident against me forever—"

"Funny how well I remembered the names you called me," she retorted. "Let's see..." She ticked off with her fingers. "I believe you called me a wimp, a damn fool, a weakling, no sense of professionalism..." She glared at him. "If case you're wondering, that's *not* the way to handle someone who's just been shattered over the loss of a patient."

"You *were* weak!" he nearly shouted, and Julia was glad it was after hours and the office was deserted. "You've got to be strong when you're a doctor, even if it is *just* a general practitioner!"

Julia raised her chin. "So it's back to *just* a general practitioner," she said, and her voice was quiet and dignified. "I can see your opinion of the field hasn't changed." Julia gathered up the files on the desk and turned to put them in the receptionist's in-box. "I'm going back to my apartment, Alex, before I say or do something that will lower me to your level. Goodnight."

****

Julia's throat was thick with tears when she got home. She hesitated, then picked up the phone and dialed Sandra Kempke's phone number in Jasper.

"Hi! I'm surprised to hear from you!" exclaimed Sandra. "How's Portland?"

"Big. Crowded. Listen, Sandra, I need to bounce some ideas off of you. Do you have a few minutes?"

"Sure. Todd's working, so I'm alone with the

baby. What's up?"

Julia poured her heart out to Sandra, expressing her fear of abandonment, her frustration with her current residency, even Robin's unhappiness.

"I don't know what to do," she wailed at last, dissolving into tears. "I miss Ben, I *know* he'd be good for me, but I'm scared to death to take a chance on him."

"Look, life is full of chances," replied Sandra. "Haven't you ever done something that you didn't think you could do? You know, take a chance and have it turn out well?"

"Yeah, sometimes..."

"Like Sara," continued Sandra. "She was scared to death to try getting pregnant again, after losing her first baby. And sure enough, it was just as bad as before. But without her courage, I would never have had the guts to get pregnant myself. And it turned out well for both of us."

Julia winced, and was thankful that Sandra couldn't see her face. It only turned out well because of Ben. Ben had saved Sandra and her baby...and the Ben had made sure Julia was prepared to save Sara and *her* baby.

She sniffed and swiped at her nose with a tissue. "You're right. I'm glad I called you, Sandra. I needed another woman to talk to."

"Hey, anytime. So..." Sandra paused with exaggerated curiosity. "Are you coming back to Jasper soon?"

Julia managed a laugh. "Maybe. I'm not sure, but maybe. Things are kind of complicated on this end, but we'll see."

"Well, think about what I said. I gotta go, the baby's crying. Stay in touch, y'hear?"

"I'll do that. And Sandra...thanks."

Julia thought long and hard about Sandra's words after she hung up.

How had she succeeded in saving Sara and her baby? By being prepared.

Maybe—just maybe—she could be prepared in terms of a long-term relationship, too. Maybe she could prepare by not *expecting* failure, but instead expecting the best... and then working to make sure the best actually happened.

Was it possible to make it work?

And for the first time, a sense of optimism bloomed inside her.

****

Julia managed to stick it out for a week before she gave up and went to talk to Dr. Schweitzer.

"What do you think about going back to Jasper, Robin?" she asked her cat, as she drank her morning coffee and prepared to go see her precept. "I have a feeling it's going to be sooner than we think."

Robin didn't rumble a purr as he ordinarily did when she scratched his neck. He hated the two rooms she was living in with the passion only cats can show. He slunk around in corners or sat sulkily on her bed, refusing to play with his new cat toys and eating very little food.

"You miss that place, don't you?" she added. She slipped on comfortable shoes and leaned down to tie the laces. "I do too. It's going to be weird for me, taking a chance like this, but I can't go on living with the thought of never seeing Ben again. Even if he doesn't want me any more, I'm going to try."

In the hospital administrative wing, Pat's secretary announced her arrive.

"Morning, Pat," said Julia, as she poked her head into the precept's office. "I need to talk with you a minute."

Pat Schweitzer looked up and laid aside a pen. "Sure, Julia. What's up?"

"I'd like to reconsider finishing up my last rotation in Jasper."

He cocked his head and was silent a moment, fiddling with the pen. "Why the sudden change in plans?" he asked at last.

"Well..." Julia seated herself and clasped her hands between her knees. "I'm sure you're aware that Alex and I were...well, *involved* prior to my departure last April. I thought things were completely over between us, but...well..."

"Alex doesn't think so?"

Relieved, Julia smiled. "I'm afraid not. He's hinting pretty broadly that I should reconsider our personal relationship."

"I hate to think that you're running away from a good residency experience just to avoid Alex, though. Do you want me to reassign you to another internist?"

Running away. There was that term again. *She* was running again, but this time she was running in the right direction. "No, thanks. First, I don't believe I'm running away," she replied. "I've come to the understanding that internal medicine isn't my interest. I far prefer trauma and deep wound laceration repair. Which, I hate to say, is far more common in Jasper than in Portland. All those loggers and farmers, you know."

"Any other reason?" asked Pat softly.

Startled at his tone, Julia looked up into the man's fatherly face. She smiled. "And there's the matter of Dr. Ben Taylor," she answered.

"I thought so." Pat Schweitzer fiddled some more with the pen on his desk. "Well, Dr. Taylor was telling me about how hard it is to attract doctors to that community. I have a feeling he'll be happy to have you back."

"Perhaps he will, professionally. With other matters...well, we'll see."

"Can I be expected to be invited to the wedding?"

She managed to chuckle. "Either that, or a

funeral. We had—words—before I left. He wasn't pleased at my decision to leave. However, I have hopes that we'll be able to reconcile.

"Good luck, then. We'll miss you here, but I think you've found your niche."

"I think so too."

"Do you want me to talk to Alex?"

"No, thanks." She grinned wolfishly. "It will give me great pleasure to talk to him myself." She held out her hand. "Thanks for being so understanding, Pat."

"No problem." He pumped her arm. "And don't forget to invite me to the wedding."

****

"What do you mean, you're leaving?"

"Just that. I'm going back to Jasper and finish my residency there."

Alex's face empurpled. "You can't tell me that being in that little backwater slime-hole is going to give you the training you need..."

"Alex, I've accomplished more in that backwater slime-hole in three months than I did in the last *year* in Portland." Julia kept her tone calm. She rather enjoyed having the upper hand over Alex. "Besides, I don't like working for you. I don't like your attitude toward your patients, I don't like your attitude toward your staff, and I don't like your attitude toward me. I'm returning to a place where the patients need me, and that's more than I can say here."

"You'll regret this, Julia..."

"Why?" She raised her chin and looked him full in the face. "Get over the blow to your ego, Alex. You're a jerk, and a first-rate one at that. Find some other resident to bully. Good-bye."

She did an about-face, snatched her purse off the desk, and walked out the door.

God, it felt good.

Chapter Eleven

Julia didn't let the Jasper Medical Clinic know she was coming back. A small, hidden, excited part of her wanted it to be a surprise.

She was as eager as a child on the long drive from Portland, Oregon to Jasper, Idaho. Beside her on the passenger seat, Robin sulked in his carrier box.

"Don't worry, you'll be home soon," she told him. "I don't know what on earth possessed me to think that you'd adapt to life in a city apartment." She thought for a moment and added, "I guess it was because for the first time I felt obligated to something. Or someone."

The idea left her thoughtful for many miles of boring highway. The words commitment, obligation, and dedication were still hard for her to accept. Yet the tug of longing toward the tiny town and its resident doctor could not be denied.

Ben. She gave a wiggle of excitement at the thought of seeing him again.

She crossed the bridge over the massive Columbia River and entered Washington. The dry, desert-like landscape of southeastern Washington gradually gave way to sparse pine woods as she drove north. She touched on Spokane, then dropped south and entered Idaho.

Ah, this was better. The rolling prairie and dense forest were welcome and familiar. How could she ever have thought this place desolate and remote? Well, remote, maybe; desolate, no.

Instead, daisies and wild roses bloomed, the oceanspray bushes were in full froth, and the sun sparkled on the glossy needles of the ponderosa pines and red firs.

Julia slowed as she approached Jasper. About a mile before she came to the town, she saw a pickup idling on a dirt road, waiting for her to pass before pulling onto the rural two-lane highway. There was something familiar about the truck. She slowed and saw that it was Clem Parker.

Impulsively she stepped on the brakes and pulled in so that her window and Clem's were close. Beside the bearded man was Jessie, properly strapped in.

"Hello, Clem!" she said.

He looked puzzled for a moment, then grinned. "Dr. Chambers!" He reached through the truck window and pumped the hand she offered. "I thought you were leaving for Portland to finish your training."

"I did go back to Portland, but I requested to finish my residency here. I'm just now coming back into town." She gave a small grimace. "Portland wasn't quite as I remember it."

He grinned. "We're glad to have you back, ma'am."

"Daddy!" Jessie tugged at his arm. "Is the pretty lady staying?"

"Yes, hon."

"Then she can come to dinner now, right?"

Clem chuckled and gave Julia an embarrassed smile. "She's got a one-track mind, this kid."

There was something so endearing about a place where children felt comfortable enough to invite doctors to dinner. "Actually, Jessie, if it's all right with your father, I'd *love* to come to dinner some time." She shifted her eyes toward Clem. "Though I don't know what my schedule will be for awhile. And

185

Ben..."

She could see Clem sum up the situation in a heartbeat. "Ben is more than welcome too. He's been out a time or two, and we've gone on some hikes."

"Has he?" Julia shook her head at her own ignorance about the man she was in love with.

"And I can show you my rock collection!" said Jessie, giving a little bounce.

"And maybe I can sew you a dress some time," Julie told the child. "Did you know I liked to sew?"

"A dress!" The girl's cheeks flushed with excitement. "Can it be red?"

"Sure."

"That's kind of you, ma'am," said Clem. A hint of sadness touched his eyes. "She hasn't had a home-made dress in some time."

"No problem. Sewing relaxes me, and I like kids." She closed her eyes for a moment. "God, it's good to be back."

Clem laughed. "I have a feeling I'm not the only one who will agree with you. Get on into town, ma'am. I suspect there's someone who will want to see you."

"Right." Julie put her car back into gear. "Nice to see you again, Clem. You too, Jessie. You can help your father decide the day I come for dinner, okay?"

Julia felt butterflies in her stomach as she pulled into the clinic parking lot.

She got out, stretched, and hoped she didn't look too frazzled after nine hours on the road. She bit her lip with excitement and walked into the clinic.

"Julia! What are you doing here!" exclaimed Lisa. The receptionist rushed around the counter to embrace Julia.

"I made arrangements with my precept in Portland to finish my residency here," said Julia.

She hugged Adele as the nurse practitioner barged into the reception area in greeting.

"But Ben didn't mention anything about it," said Adele.

"He didn't know," confessed Julia. "I was hoping to surprise him."

"Well, you will. When he gets in, that is."

Julia hid the disappointment that went through her. "He's not here?"

"No, he's out on a farm accident. He called and said the man had a broken tibia with muscle damage. He's bringing him in as soon as he can stabilize him. I'm preparing the OR, but why don't you go join him? I imagine he could use some help."

"Maybe I'll do that. Lisa, can you write down directions on how to get there? I want to change clothes first. And if you don't mind, I'll leave my cat here. He can hang around in my office until I get back."

Julia left Lisa and Adele to fuss and coo over the cat as she dashed out of her street clothes and into some comfortable work clothes.

"He's not far out of town," said Adele, handing Julia a piece of paper. "Two miles north, follow the first dirt road on the right for about a quarter mile, a blue farmhouse."

Julia climbed back in the car and drove out of town. But the butterflies of anticipation in her stomach overshadowed thoughts of the medical situation.

She couldn't wait to see Ben again. Couldn't wait to surprise him. Couldn't wait to see the look on his face when he saw her...

****

The day was beautiful and warm, with the sun arching in a cloudless sky. But Ben didn't like setting bones in the great outdoors, no matter how lovely the scenery.

He had his hands full. Stan Barclay had gotten himself tangled up in the PTO shaft of his tractor, and the family was hysterical about all the blood.

"Debra, you're going to have to *calm down*," he snapped to Stan's wife. "Why don't you and the kids go inside? It's making my job harder, having you all hanging around."

Since the kids ranged in age from three to seven, he thought this was a reasonable request. But Debra, either from misplaced concern about her husband or pure enjoyment of the drama, seemed determined to hover. The children were either staring with horrified fascination at their father's mangled leg, or crying.

"Easy, Stan," murmured Ben. "You've lost a fair bit of blood—don't keep thrashing or you'll get that femoral artery going again."

"Damn, but it hurts, Doc."

"Of course it does. Okay, listen. Now that I've got the bleeding under control, I'm going to numb you from the hips down. You might lose bladder control, just to warn you, but it's either that or go through the pain as I set this leg. At least the bone break is clean, which is more than I can say about the muscle."

Stan was panting fast, his eyes glazed and his skin clammy. Ben had treated him for shock, and he was just starting to respond. At the news that he might lose bladder control, however, he started to move in protest....then moaned at the pain in his leg. "Okay, doc, whatever you have to do."

"That's my man. Okay, here goes. Debra, would you *please* take the kids and go into the house? Neither you nor they should have to see this." But Debra still hovered.

Ben numbed Stan's leg and prepared to set the bone. "I'll set it properly when we're at the clinic, but this will stabilize it and make you more comfortable until I get you there," he told Stan. He looked at the torn up muscles in Stan's thigh, and recalled Jake

Smothers' injury. "Damn, I wish Julia were here," he muttered.

"Be careful what you wish for," said a voice. "It might come true."

Ben whirled. "Julia!" Was she a dream? Was he imagining things?

"In person." She smiled.

Ben didn't care how serious Stan's injury was. To him, the world had just brightened to a blinding degree. She looked beautiful, stunning, radiant...

From beside him, Stan said, "Doc?" No answer. "Doc? *Ben?*"

"What?" He blinked himself back to reality and looked at Stan.

"Uh, I hate to break this up, but I'm in pain here."

"Oh. Right. Sorry."

Julia knelt beside him. "What's the situation?"

He felt dizzy with love and relief, and had to shake his head to clear his brain and answer her question. "Open fracture of the tibia, lots of muscle damage. I've just numbed him from the hips down, but we need to get this bone stabilized until we can get him to the clinic."

"What do you have as a splint?"

"That." Ben waved to a broomstick lying nearby.

Julia nodded. "First things first, though." She rose and headed towards Debra Barclay and the children, and Ben watched in gratitude as she spoke to the woman and shepherded the family across the yard to the house.

"Hell of a woman," he murmured, and turned his attention to Stan.

Julia returned, and together they splinted Stan's leg to the broomstick, and then Julia held Stan immobile while Ben applied steady, strong traction to pull the bone ends apart. Despite the numbness, Stan breathed a sigh of relief when the bones slid into place.

"That's better," Ben murmured. "Okay, Julia, let's get him to the clinic. Stan, we're going to slide you onto this stretcher and take you in."

Before driving away, though, Ben yanked Julia toward him, planted a kiss on her lips, and then climbed into his vehicle.

In ten minutes, the clinic was full to bursting. Debra Barclay and the three children milled around the waiting room, either crying or talking loudly. Ben, Julia, and Adele had Stan in the clinic's small operating room, cutting away his jeans and cleaning the wound.

"Feel up to stitching?" Ben asked Julia.

"Sure."

Adele prepared the materials while Julia scrubbed. Ben watched her every move, unable to believe she was here, with him, working together again.

"Easy, cowboy," murmured Adele, too softly for Julia to hear.

Ben smiled. "A happy doctor is a good doctor."

"Happy, yes. Delirious, no."

Julia came over to the operating table and picked up a needle. "Here we go."

Ben watched her skillful stitching. No doubt about it—the woman had talent. "When you said you liked to sew," he commented, "I thought you meant on fabric."

"I love this part of medicine," she replied, tying off a knot. "Taking broken tissue and putting it all back together. Makes it all worthwhile."

"So glad to hear it," muttered Stan. He kept his eyes firmly on the wall.

Within an hour, Stan's leg was as repaired as they could manage. Ben and Julia applied the cast, then Julia left to talk to Debra while Ben prepared Stan for what to expect during his recovery.

"You're going to be in some pain for awhile, Stan," said Ben, stripping off his latex gloves. "I'm going to write you a prescription for some painkillers. Can Debra get into Moscow to pick it up today or tomorrow?"

"Yeah, probably. But Doc—how will I get around?"

"I think you should be on crutches," said Ben. "Unless you want to take over my old wheelchair."

Stan made a face. "Not if I can help it. I saw what you went through."

"Fortunately I had Julia to help me through the last part of it. Trying to run a clinic while sitting down wasn't easy."

Stan looked around. "Where is she?"

"Talking to your wife. She'll be back soon."

Stan grinned. "Granted I was a little out of it with pain, but didn't I hear you say something when she showed up at my place? Something about being a hell of a woman?"

"You got it." Ben smiled.

Stan waggled his eyebrows. "Is there more to this than meets the eye?"

"Just use your imagination, man. It's my plan that she'll never leave."

****

Julia fetched Robin from her office, stuffed him back in his travel box, and drove to the little rental house she had left less than two weeks ago.

She never thought she'd see it again, yet here it stood, more welcoming than she could imagine. In the front yard, she opened up the box and released the cat.

He knew where he was immediately. Without much ado, he trotted toward the backyard and his favorite haunts.

Julia followed, knowing that the back door would be unlocked as she had left it. She walked in, threw open all the doors and windows to the sweet summer air, and waited.

She knew Ben would come.

Within half an hour he came bursting through the open front door and grabbed her in a bear hug.

"You came back," he murmured into her neck. "You came back."

"Yes." She pulled back just far enough to look into his eyes, surprised to find them moist.

"You didn't tell me!"

"I wanted to surprise you." She grinned. "Did it work?"

"Yes!" He looped his arms over her shoulder and touched his forehead to hers. "I nearly fell over in surprise. There I am with poor Stan at my feet, broken leg and ripped up muscles, and I felt this rainbow of happiness explode in my chest."

"Good. That was my plan. I felt like a kid about to open a Christmas present, knowing that you'd be surprised." She grinned. "It's what kept me going on that long trip from Portland."

Ben released her and led her to the sofa. "But why are you here at all?"

"I'm here to finish my residency. I found that working for Alex was every bit as bad as you predicted. That, and I had a conversation with Sandra Kempke that put my head on straight." She tightened her arms. "I'm glad to be here again. I missed you. It seems like *ages* since I left."

"It has been. Julia, are you here *just* to finish your residency? Or are you here for longer?"

"Longer, if you'll have me. I seem to have lost my taste for life in Portland. And as for Robin, well, he *hated* it there."

"Good for Robin. *Really* good for Robin."

He pulled her into the crook of his arm. Julia was happy to snuggle against him. "God, I've missed you," she murmured.

Ben leaned his head down and kissed her.

Minutes later, when they came up for air, Julia knew the time had come to clear things up between them.

"Okay, confession time," she said.

"Confession about what?"

"Me. I need to explain a few things, especially things like why I insisted on leaving Jasper despite the fact that there wasn't any reason for me to go back to Portland."

"Is this a long story?"

"Yes."

"Then let's go to my place and be comfortable. I'll make us some coffee."

Julia smiled. "Will we be going to bed together before or after the story?"

He grinned back. "After. I want to hear the story, but yes...I have no doubt we'll end up in bed."

Julia felt a thrill of anticipation run through her stomach as they walked out of the house, hand-in-hand. "I'll leave Robin here for now," she said. "I think he's anxious to re-acquaint himself with the backyard."

They walked to Ben's house hand-in-hand. Halfway there, they turned a corner and saw Sara.

She wore a baby sling with her newborn close to her chest. When she saw Julia, she stopped in her tracks. "Julia!"

"Sara." Julia rushed forward, and the women embraced with the infant between them.

"You're back."

"Yes, I'm back. And I'm staying."

Sara sniffed and blinked hard. "I'm so glad. *So* glad. Sandra mentioned how unhappy you were in Portland."

"It was Sandra who convinced me that I should come back."

"Remind me to thank her."

"Let me see the baby."

Sara pulled the fabric of the sling away, and Julia peered inside. "Oh Sara, she's beautiful…"

"Yes, and healthy too. Thanks to you."

Julia felt the sting of moisture in her eyes. It occurred to her that she would be around to watch this baby grow up. What a concept. What a *great* concept.

"Mary Elaine," she murmured, recalling the baby's name. "You're a lucky woman, Sara."

"Well." Sara readjusted the sling and glanced at Ben. "Maybe you'll have one of your own someday."

Julia chuckled. "Maybe I will."

****

The inside of Ben's house was the same: the walls of books, the rural prints on the walls, the pile of soiled socks in the corner. Gypsy launched herself at Julia with such force that Julia staggered back, laughing. She spent the few minutes it took Ben to make coffee scratching Gypsy's ears.

"The coffee's on, but it will stay hot for awhile." Ben grabbed Julia around the waist. "First there are other things I want to do."

"I thought you said you wanted to hear the story first."

"I changed my mind."

Julia laughed and kicked off her shoes.

****

Their lovemaking was fierce and sweet.

Julia was the aggressor, trying to convey to Ben her joy in being back, in being in his arms again. And she was.

Her fears were laid to rest. How could she think about professional worries with Ben's utter confidence in her abilities? How could she think about Alex's betrayal with Ben's mouth devastating her senses? How could she think about abandonment when Ben's body was joined with hers?

They lay together afterwards, holding hands, talking in quiet voices. And Julia nearly wept with the relief and gladness to be back

****

Later, dressed only in one of Ben's oversized shirts, Julia propped her feet up on his coffee table and sipped her coffee.

"Don't you have to get back to the clinic?" she asked.

"Lisa will call me if I'm needed." He dropped a kiss on her shoulder. "I deserve a couple of hours off."

"Hmmm." She raised her face and they lingered over each other for a few moments.

"So tell me what happened in Portland," demanded Ben.

Julia chuckled. "It was awful from beginning to end." She told him about the traffic, about how unhappy Robin was in her apartment, how she had discovered the superiority of the coffee at Betty's Café. "It seemed like my whole viewpoint changed," she admitted. "The things I had loved about Portland a few months ago had lost their appeal."

"It's like I said earlier, you're a small-town girl at heart and just didn't want to admit it."

"You're right."

"So…what happened with Alex?"

Julia groaned. "Oh man, you have no idea. I'd forgotten all those little quirks of his that drove me nuts. That way he laughs in his superior manner. The way he elevates an eyebrow to signify disapproval. The way he always assumes he's right, no matter what. His general disdain for people. It's funny, I had never appreciated how much a GP needs to be a people person. You need a personal touch with your patients. Alex lacks that big time."

"What did he think of the training you'd

received here?"

"I don't think he cared. He just wanted to get me back in bed."

Bed stroked her thigh. "Did he succeed?" he asked with a smile.

"Are you kidding? Not by a long shot. After knowing *you*, how can you ask such a question?"

Ben chuckled. "I wasn't too worried."

"I also realized another thing about Alex that bugged me. He doesn't think I can succeed as a doctor without his mentoring and support."

"Oh, he's one of *those*."

"Yes. It was funny—we were in the hospital cafeteria one day when Pat Schweitzer came by, and he started telling Alex all about Sara's complications and how I'd saved her. Alex was bug-eyed under Pat's diatribe. I'm sure Pat did it on purpose."

"I like this guy Pat. I hope I can meet him some day."

"Pat's always had faith in me. But anyway, the fact that I'd obviously gained both experience and confidence in this little backwater clinic drove Alex nuts. But it was my conversation with Sandra that finally cleared my brain."

"You saw Sandra?"

"No, I called her. In tears, I might add. I told her how scared I was to take a chance with you, and she told me life was full of chances. How she took the chance to get pregnant again despite the fact that her sister lost her first baby. It made me realize how cowardly I'd been, not to face my fears."

"That's the funny thing," said Ben. "You *have* been facing your fears. What you did with Sara was nothing short of fabulous, and you overcame your fears beautifully."

"Maybe. But it's a lot easier to face professional fears than it is personal fears."

"So what's with the personal fears? Why are you

196

afraid to take chances on people?"

"Because the people in my life have always left me." She told him her sad history of parental abandonment. "It didn't matter that I was attractive. No one ever stuck around because of that." She added on a bitter note, "Including Alex."

Ben took her hand.

"So that's why I was so fiercely determined to make it as a doctor," continued Julia. "That's something I *could* control—that couldn't be taken away from me. Until I lost that pre-eclamptic patient last January, that is. Then suddenly there was something to fear—losing another patient to the same condition."

"Are you still frightened about pre-eclamptic patients?"

Julie shook her head. "How can I be?"

"And how about your fears that I'll abandon you?"

Julie looked at him, saw the laugh lines around his eyes, felt the warmth of his hand on hers. "You committed yourself to staying in Jasper to be its doctor. You helped me through Sara's case. You're a rock in this town, Ben. You've been *my* rock. So..." She smiled shyly. "Until you do something to the contrary, I guess I can take you at your word."

He lifted her hand and dropped a kiss on it.

"Did you ever listen to Simon & Garfunkel?" asked Julia.

"Sure."

"Do you remember the words to *I am a Rock*?"

"I think so." Ben started to sing, "A winter's day..."

"Those are the words I lived by," interrupted Julia. "I have no need of friendship, friendship causes pain, it's laughter and it's loving I disdain..."

Ben winced. "Your whole life?"

"Pretty much. *Hiding in my room, safe within*

my womb, I touch no one and no one touches me. That's what I did. That's why Sandra and Sara were a chink in my armor—I felt such a draw of friendship for them. And now you..." She leaned over and planted a kiss on his lips. "You made all the difference. Because I found I didn't like being an island that never cries."

"And you're no longer an island?"

"No. At least..." She smiled impishly. "Maybe I'm a peninsula or something. I thought of something else after talking with Sandra too."

"What's that?"

"That maybe I've been going into relationships *prepared* to fail, in order to protect myself when the inevitable happened. To never relax and go with the flow. So I'm here to try something new—I'm going to *prepare* to succeed." Her hand tightened on his. "I won't be good at it at first. But I love you, Ben—and I want to stay."

"It won't be an easy life, you know—running the clinic by ourselves."

"We ran it for three months and did fine."

"But what about...later?"

"Later?"

"Hang on, I just remembered something."

He jumped up from the couch and hurried into the bedroom while Julia stared after him in bemusement. In a moment he was back.

He went down on one knee in front of her. "Now I finally have the chance to ask you something I've wanted for a long time."

Julia's heart started pounding.

He fished a tiny box out of his pocket and snapped it open. "Julia, will you marry me?"

Julia's eyes dropped to the sparkly diamond ring, then rose to Ben's eyes. They sparkled brighter than the diamond. Her throat thickened. "Oh Ben..."

"I know you're anxious about the future...

"Ben..."

"And you have those fears of commitment and all that..."

"Ben..."

"And that you have concerns that I'll leave you someday..."

"Ben!"

"What?

"The answer is *yes*."

Ben's shoulders wilted as if with relief. He grinned. "Really?"

"Really."

He catapulted up and yanked her to her feet to embrace her. "Thank God," he whispered into her neck.

Julia laughed and pulled back. "Were you really afraid I'd say no?"

"The thought had occurred to me."

"I'm happy to prove you wrong." She kissed him.

His embrace tightened. "So...how well does Robin get along with dogs?"

Epilogue

"Okay, now push. Pu-u-u-u-ush. That's it, good."

Julia panted and caught her breath. Sweat trickled down her temples as she labored to bring forth her child into Ben's waiting hands. "Here comes another contraction," she whispered as the pain gathered.

"All right, honey...yes, here it comes..."

All of her muscles bunched as her body contracted. Adele, the nurse, stood by as she held Julia's clenched hand. A moan escaped her lips until she caught her breath and pushed with all her might.

Ben, his face masked and a surgical cap over his hair, sat on a stool by her feet. Nearby were the instruments to help sever the cord that would bring his child into the world.

Julia gritted her teeth at the strain as she pushed.

"I can see the head," exclaimed Ben. "One more push, Julia."

But Julia lay back, exhausted, unable to continue for a moment. Adele wiped the sweat from her forehead.

Ben laid a hand on her protruding stomach, feeling the muscles, waiting for the next contraction.

"It'll be the next one, I think," said Julia.

"I think so too. Just a bit more, Julia, then the worst will be over."

"At least I'm not pre-eclamptic," she quipped, then caught her breath as the next contraction started and the pain intensified. "Here it goes..."

Ben dropped back down on the stool. "That's it...good...here's the head..." He reached down and delicately caught the head of his first-born child, turning it and clearing mucus out of the mouth.

Julia felt a guttural, primitive growl escape her throat as she gave one last mighty push. With a deflating sensation and an immediate ceasing of pain, she pushed the baby out.

"It's a girl!" exclaimed Ben. His voice was ragged, and lifting her head Julia saw that her husband's face was wet with tears.

"A girl," she said, and laughed through her own tears. "Our own sweet girl, Ben."

Adele laughed too; in the thick teary voice that Julia had come to know meant that the older woman was close to crying.

Ben clamped and cut the umbilical cord, then laid the baby on a warming table while Adele finished suctioning the airway. Then she wrapped the infant in a towel and handed her to Ben. "Congratulations."

Ben took the infant in awe. Julia could see it on his face—the dawning love, the new sense of parental responsibility, the realization that this baby was his—his and hers...

"Look at her, Julia," said Ben. "Isn't she gorgeous?"

He laid the bundle on her chest, and Julia looked into the red wrinkled face of her child. "Anne Lucille Taylor. Oh Ben, she's beautiful."

"Contraction," interrupted Adele.

"Oh yeah," said Ben with a grin. "I guess I'd better help you finish this business."

Julia hardly noticed the contractions that began to expel the placenta from her body. She was too absorbed in studying the minute face in her arms.

In ten minutes it was over, the delivery

complete, and Adele cleaned Julia up. Then she left the new parents alone for some minutes of privacy. Ben yanked the stool over next to Julia and gazed at the baby.

"I can't believe it," he breathed. "A girl. Look at her. I feel like my soul is shaking or something. I read that description once in a book, and it's never been more real to me. Of all the babies I've delivered, this one is *ours!*"

Julia smiled at his enthusiasm. "It's a good thing we managed to lure another doctor to this town," she said. "With Erik on duty for the next week, you can take time to become acquainted with Anne."

Ben dropped a kiss on Julia's mouth. "After two years running this clinic with you, I thought I would object to having another doctor around. Now I'm glad he's here."

"Once I get back on my feet we'll have to figure out a working schedule around a parenting schedule. God, Ben, she's beautiful…"

"Just like her mother."

Julia grinned the giddy grin of a new mother. "I feel like I'm flying," she admitted. "Up on cloud nine. Like I could dance!"

"Not unless you want to start hemorrhaging. Can I hold her?"

Julia handed the precious bundle to her husband. He cradled the infant, absorbing her, memorizing her.

Julie sniffed. She couldn't help it.

Ben jerked his head up. "What's wrong? Are you in pain?"

"No. It's not that." She laughed and wiped away a tear. "It's just that…well, you're beautiful, Ben. The way you're looking at her. God, I'm so happy…"

He grinned. "None of those fears you used to have materialized, have they?"

202

"I can hardly remember what they are." She reached out and touched Ben's cheek lightly. "And now it seems like all my dreams have come true."

"See? I told you I was right," said Ben smugly. "I knew you'd make a country doctor one day."

"And a country wife. And now a country mother."

Ben leaned over and dropped a kiss on her mouth. "I love you, Julia."

Thank you for purchasing this Wild Rose Press publication. For other wonderful stories of romance, please visit our on-line bookstore at www.thewildrosepress.com.

For questions or more information contact us at info@thewildrosepress.com.

The Wild Rose Press
www.TheWildRosePress.com

LaVergne, TN USA
24 September 2009
158940LV00001B/59/P